BEGIN WHERE WE ARE

DIANA KNIGHTLEY

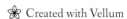

For Kevin, it's in the breaths between the words...

PART I
MAGNUS AND KAITLYN

MAGNUS

*I*t was just before dawn when I kissed her for the last time and slipped away.

The hospital was quiet. Nurses watched me curiously as I found my way tae the exit doors.

Quentin was asleep in the car outside and startled awake when I climbed in. "Hey Boss, how's Katie? Man, it's still dark out — going home for something? I could pick it up for you?"

"Kaitlyn is as well as can be expected. She will be released this morning. But I..." I took a deep breath tae get through the next words. "I will already be gone."

"Oh. That sucks."

"Aye Master Quentin, I need a ride home tae gather my things."

"Katie is going to be... whoa — this is really not good."

"Aye. But there is nae other way. I need ye tae take care of her tae make sure she is safe. I daena ken what danger there is, but up tae now it has been devastating. She will need a friend and a protector. I hope ye will remain with her and be both."

Quentin nodded, fiddling with the keys in the ignition. "Yeah, of course. Yeah." He started the car and pulled it from the parking lot.

I leaned on the door and shielded my eyes with a hand. "I daena think the house is safe."

"I don't know, Boss, I can tighten security measures. Hire more men..."

"Tis nae enough. I daena ken what will happen next but if I am at odds with Lady Mairead, and I will be, she may well come for Kaitlyn. I spoke with Kaitlyn about it, she is willing tae go tae the apartments."

"Oh, sure, that could work."

Quentin took a sharp turn. I pulled in some more air. My chest felt tight — a familiar constrictin' that came on as a fight was nearing. With my eyes clamped shut I said, "The move will need tae happen today. Kaitlyn needs tae go directly there. I daena want her tae go tae the house."

"Yes, Boss. What about Zach and Emma?"

"They need tae move as well, by tonight."

Quentin pulled the car up tae the house. "You're sure about this? I mean, there's nothing else that can be done? I don't know, I don't know how Katie will survive."

I clenched my jaw. "Every action I take is tae keep Kaitlyn alive. I daena need your questioning, I need your assurances. Will ye protect her and get her tae safety?"

"Yes. Of course I will."

"Good. I am countin' on ye."

"Where will you be and when will you be back?"

"I will be fulfillin' my vow. Tis no sense in plannin' because I am unlikely tae return."

"Oh, that's really..."

I sat for a moment grasping air and pulling it into my chest.

"Aye." Then I opened the car door and headed toward my house for the last time.

"Is Katie with you?" Chef Zach was looking over the stair railing when I entered.

"Nae, she will be released in a few hours." I leaned on the kitchen counter. "I need breakfast, Chef Zach—"

He jogged down the steps to the kitchen. "Definitely."

"Will ye send Emma tae be there when Kaitlyn is released?"

Chef Zach stopped with his hand on the refrigerator door. "Where will you be?"

"I will be gone." I stood straighter. "You will be helpin' Quentin tae move your family and Kaitlyn tae the apartments today." This was easier tae say if I stared out the sliding doors while sayin' it. "I want this house closed up by nightfall."

Chef Zach looked from me tae Quentin. "All right Magnus, sure, but Katie..."

"Aye, but Kaitlyn. There is nothin' else but Kaitlyn. Tis all there is. Yet I must go anyway." I crossed the living room for our bedroom and paused at the door. "I expect she will need a great many friends about her..."

Chef Zach pulled a dozen eggs from the refrigerator and put them on the counter. "Yeah, she will."

Emma stood at the top of the stairs, "You're leaving Katie?"

I clenched my jaw. "Aye. I am leavin'. I need tae—" I had been talkin' about this for too long. I needed tae leave. Every moment was a danger tae these people. What would happen if Lady Mairead knew Kaitlyn lost the baby? And how long before she knew? I needed tae move fast and arrive before she learned the truth of it. Without our bairn my vow had nae power behind it.

She would hold Kaitlyn against me.

And time was passing.

"Chef Zach, I need breakfast in a hurry. Will ye inform Emma of my instructions?"

"Yes, I will. Eggs, bacon, and coffee coming in a second."

MAGNUS

I dressed in a kilt. There was a bowl of shark teeth Kaitlyn kept near our bed. I sifted through it in search of the largest and added it tae my sporran.

I collapsed back on the bed and tried tae get my breathin' right.

This bed I shared with Kaitlyn. This room. This house. I attempted tae slow my breaths with a deep intake. Then with as much composure as I could gather I left the bed and then the room.

I ate breakfast by myself. I told Zach I dinna want company and that he and Quentin should begin tae pack. Quentin was on his phone arrangin' for a truck and Zach and Emma were movin' around upstairs getting ready for a busy day. I ate my breakfast starin' at a fixed point in front of my eyes, chewin' slowly. I wanted tae relish this meal, but I couldna taste it. Twas stuffin' under my constricted chest.

Emma came down when I was finishin' the last bite. "Magnus, I rarely, if ever, question you but I don't understand. Why do you have to go?"

"Tis enough that Kaitlyn understands."

"I mean, yeah, but still — Zach and I will be the ones trying to help her through this, at least give me a reason so I can understand."

I pushed my plate away. "Madame Emma, I have done everythin' in my power tae keep Kaitlyn safe but I haena been enough. In every calculation I have been mistaken. Tis because I am trying tae win. I wanted to beat Lord Delapointe, so I allowed Kaitlyn to risk her life. I have been at odds with Lady Mairead and she has threatened Kaitlyn's life over and over. I am goin' tae stop tryin' tae win."

"So you aren't trying to win? You're just losing?"

"I am nae tryin' tae win. I am tryin' tae keep Kaitlyn alive."

"But you love her and she just lost the baby and..."

"I canna leave her, Madame Emma. Yet I have tae go. I made a vow, my life for her's. I can only leave an empty house. Tis the only way I can go."

Emma watched me and then nodded. "I'm going to go to the hospital. It's been really great working for you. I mean that. I hope you come home."

I concentrated on that spot again, the one just above my plate, while she grabbed her bag and keys and left.

Zach came downstairs. "Quentin has a truck on the way, plus two more movers." He paused just about where Emma was standin' moments before. "I'm not good at goodbyes..."

"I am nae good at them either, Chef Zach. I hope twill suffice tae say, I will miss your cookin' verra much."

"That suffices, thanks Magnus." He crossed tae the cabinets, opened a box of protein bars, and poured them out on the table.

"I think this will fit in your bag? Take them so you don't starve, at least not in the first two days."

I picked up a handful and added them tae my sporran.

Zach said, "I'm going to go upstairs to finish packing." He returned tae his rooms.

I went tae the office and opened the safe tae retrieve the vessel. I sat in the chair and considered leavin' Kaitlyn a note — but how tae put words tae the moment? I couldna pick up the writing instrument tae begin because there wasna a beginning.

I was only faced with the end and it seemed too brutal tae say.

I returned downstairs and through the sliding door tae the deck.

Quentin turned as I approached. "Boss, I wanted to say good-bye, I — you know, thanks for taking a chance on me. It meant a lot. I just wanted you to know that."

"Master Quentin ye never proved me wrong. Thank ye for keepin' her safe. You have done a better job than I most days."

"You sure you don't need me to go with you? I've gotten pretty good with a sword, I could...?"

His voice trailed off when I shook my head. "I have tae do this alone. I canna worry over keepin' ye alive, whether ye are good with a blade or nae."

"But I am good with the sword, right?"

"Aye, ye are good. But I need ye tae stay here and take care of Kaitlyn."

"All right then. Cool. Next time you'll take me."

I stared out at the horizon.

"Okay Magnus, see ya soon." He turned and walked back to the house.

I took another deep breath, twisted the ends of the vessel, aligned the markings, and as it glowed tae life I began tae count. "One, naught, three, twenty..."

And the brutal assault on my body began.

MAGNUS

*I*lumbered up into a sitting position and tried tae remain conscious. Unnnggghhhhhh. Unnnggghhh-hhh. My jaw clenched against the spasms.

This forest was nae far from Talsworth where I would turn myself over tae Lady Mairead.

Did I want Lady Mairead to have my vessel?

Twas the only one I possessed and possibly the only one I would ever...

I would need tae hide it in a location where it could be found again.

A memory flashed — the stone wall, the tree, shewin' Kaitlyn how they aligned with the tower. I forced myself tae my feet with a groan and took stock of my location.

I needed another hour tae rest before I would be well enough tae accomplish this, but I dinna have the time. I had tae move fast.

I staggered forward with the help of tree branches and leanin' against rocks tae rest until I arrived at the tree I was looking for. The tower was aligned. Eight steps away stood the low wall. The corner was well stacked and looked as if it would stand for many long years.

I found a rock with a sharp edge, crawled over the wall, knelt in the corner, and began tae dig at the difficult ground until I gained a hole deep enough.

I dropped the vessel in and covered it with dirt. Then I brought more dirt from the surrounding area and created a berm up the corner. I covered the slope with rocks tae stabilize and hide it. I covered that with leaves and detritus from the nearby trees. When I stepped back tae check twas well hidden from view.

I dinna want tae take a chance of gettin' captured this close tae it, so I stepped over the wall, walked south, and leaned against an oak. Facing the direction of the castle, I ate a protein bar in peanut-butter flavor, and then I ate another.

Twas afternoon. Now that I accomplished this without capture I regretted I dinna go tae Balloch first. I would have liked tae see Lizbeth and Sean before I left.

I dug a small hole, put the protein bar wrappers into it, and buried them under a small mound of dirt. I looked at my handiwork and brushed what dirt I could get from my hands. They were filthy. It only took about two hours tae look as if I belonged in the eighteenth century.

I straightened my shirt and kilt and strode tae the edge of the field. There, I leaned on a tree in full view of the castle and waited for the Talsworth guard tae come get me. What was left of the Talsworth guard, we Campbells crushed them quite brutally nae long ago. We had left just a few men standing, nae enough tae cause trouble with us anymore.

After that battle I had returned tae the woods victorious and that was when I found Kaitlyn gone.

I had promised tae take care of her, tae protect her, and she disappeared while I was fighting. I shook my head tryin' tae clear the image of her backpack lyin' open beside Rory's body. And then the hours and days lookin' for her, knowin' any moment she might die. They were verra long hours.

I remembered my words when I found her—

"I have one purpose in life, tae keep ye safe, and I haena been able tae do it."

The Talsworth guards rode from the gates headed my way.

MAGNUS

*L*ady Mairead leveled her eyes. "Drop tae your knees, Magnus."

The ground was cold, hard stone.

"And why are ye here? You were nae expected for two more moons." She relaxed in a chair languidly waving her hand as she spoke.

"Kaitlyn has lost our bairn."

Her gaze snapped to mine. "Oh? I would think her physicians would be better at healing than that."

I decided nae tae answer.

"That is distressing. I suppose ye are quite broken about it? When did it happen?"

"Yesterday."

"Ah. She is still fresh with the loss and yet ye kneel here. Tis a cold manner about ye I dinna suspect." A malicious smile spread across her face.

"I assured ye that I would come tae protect my family. You and I have a deal tae that end. But I dinna ken ye would extend the protection tae Kaitlyn as she is—"

"Barren?"

"The doctors said she may soon try tae have another—"

"But nae with ye, Magnus, because ye winna be there." She leveled her gaze and added, "I imagine this has been a verra difficult day for ye, but I am glad ye have come without more discussion. All this conversation is wearing thin as a moth-eaten tapestry."

She watched my face.

"And I wouldna worry over Kaitlyn, she is a verra capable woman. She will find another husband tae protect her. I winna need tae involve her anymore because without providing an heir to us she has become insignificant."

A growl escaped from my chest.

She made a clucking noise then huffed. "Well, I suppose it canna be helped that ye are presenting yourself tae your father without an heir. Tis quite important tae him, ye ken. But there will be more wives, more opportunities tae gain his favor."

"Lady Mairead I would appreciate an end tae this part of the discussion. I have left Kaitlyn as ye asked. I have presented myself as ye commanded. I have little power in this, but I respectfully ask ye tae refrain of speaking of my wife, Kaitlyn Campbell, anymore."

She watched me slowly then stiffly nodded. "My guards said they found ye without your time-vessel? Where is it?"

"I daena ken. Once I awoke twas nae with me. I believe it has been stolen." I stared straight ahead at her left hand.

"You winna tell me where ye have hidden it?"

"Nae. Twas nae my doing."

"This complicates things because I would like tae offer ye a nice bed with a big dinner before we journey tae your father's court. But ye are nae bein' forthright with me on this matter. And ye well might steal away..."

She seemed tae contemplate it for a few moments then said,

"Guards show him tae the dungeons but I need him uninjured on the morrow when we travel."

"May I stand? I will go with the guards freely. I am ready tae travel whenever ye are ready tae go."

She waved her hand dismissing me. I stood and walked between two guards tae one of the cells in the lower part of the castle.

Kaitlyn was walking on the beach at the edge of the water, her head bowed, her hair streamin' behind her. The sun was going low but still shone on the tips of the strands. This was a familiar view — the curve of her head, the stillness of her movements, her concentration and purpose. She bent and sifted through the shells searching for shark teeth. She scooped up a handful of wee shells and then sprinkled them back to the sand. Then she moved tae the next promisin' area. And I felt fortunate, in this sparklin' sunset and beautiful landscape, tae watch her as she moved.

There would be a moment when she would realize I was standing on the end of the deck. She would pull her gaze from the sand and look up. And across. And she would smile as if she had been waitin' for me. Her face lightin' up—

So I stood on the deck and waited for her tae turn.

I raised my hand.

And then I called, "Kaitlyn!"

Her stillness dinna change. She dinna look.

"Kaitlyn!"

I tried tae run tae her, but I couldna move. All I could do was call across the beach for her, trying tae get her tae turn tae me — "Kaitlyn!"

"Kaitlyn!"

I woke with a rush of air clutching my chest. "Och." The bed was a cold stone slab. Torturous tae sleep on but I wouldna be tryin' tae sleep again.

I leaned against the wall and tried like I had been tryin' all day tae get on top of my breathin'.

I was offered an oatmeal brose for breakfast while sitting in my cell. Finally, after long hours of cold damp air and darkness and nothing much tae do but keep my mind blank so I wouldna despair, Lady Mairead appeared.

She spoke through the door. "Magnus, I will need a few more days before I am able tae leave." She paused tae wait for an answer but I was unable tae come up with anythin' tae say.

Four days. That was how long she kept me waitin' in the prison. Each night I half-slept because when I did sleep I woke with nightmares. Every night the nightmare was the same — Kaitlyn, her head turned down. She wouldna look at me when I called her name.

"Magnus, gather your things we will journey today." My entire body was stiff and unused. I stretched and stared at the door waiting for the guards tae open the lock. When I stepped into the hallway, there was barely any light.

Lady Mairead said, "You look like a bear, and ye have a smell that is verra offensive."

"Aye, it has been a long wait. I arrived here under the impression ye wanted me in better health than this."

"I did, but there's nothin' tae be done with it, ye will have tae go as you are. The guards will attend us tae the field and we will journey tae your father's court. Twill be a long journey, the worst of them all."

"I dinna ken they had a difference."

"I like tae break the journeys up with a rest in the middle. Tis why I usually have chosen Florida. Shorter distances I have found tae be almost bearable. Almost. But this time we will journey all the way tae your father's court." I fell into line behind her. Four guards accompanied us carrying large bundles. "Your father advised me tae break the distance intae pieces, but I dinna ken where the stops would be, ye dinna seem tae want tae stop in Florida, for instance. Tis verra complicated tae plan tae arrive in a strange place and time."

She spoke like this about the pain and the complications and the plannin' that went into the journey the entire time we walked. "So after deliberating we will jump the entire distance."

I stopped listenin' after she made the first point: Twould be painful. The worst so far.

We set out across the wide fields and then she commanded the guards tae leave our side. The guards deposited their bundles around her feet and left.

She dropped her skirt hem to cover the sacks. "I have been collecting," she informed me. "I need ye tae understand I winna have ye causing trouble."

"If I cause trouble what will happen tae me?"

"It's nae yourself that ye would need tae be worried for."

"Exactly. I am nae going tae cause trouble. I am simply going tae do what needs tae be done."

Her eyes squinted.

She said, "Until ye met Kaitlyn Sheffield we were nae at odds."

"Her name is Kaitlyn Campbell and we daena need tae discuss her. We arna at odds now."

"Good."

"When we arrive will there be an immediate danger? Somethin' I need tae be ready for?"

"Nae, tis quite civilized. Cover your ears, I daena want ye tae ken the numbers."

I clamped m'hands over my ears and went as still and blank as I could tae prepare for the journey. Lady Mairead stood beside me and twisted the ends of the vessel alignin' the numbers until they glowed. She kept the vessel facin' away so I couldna make sense of it. Then her lips were movin' as she spoke the numbers. She clasped a hand around my upper arm, and a moment later the agony began—

KAITLYN

I was sitting on the bed waiting for a nurse to bring my release paperwork. Hayley bustled in full of pep and business but then she softened. "Hey sweetie, you get to go home now?"

"Not home. Apparently Quentin and Zach are moving me into an apartment, but yeah, I get to go." I finished, "I can totally walk out on my own two feet, but they want me to ride in a wheelchair."

"It's protocol." She put her purse down on the chair and sat beside me on the bed. "Emma is outside with Ben waiting in the car. She told me Magnus left."

I nodded and sniffled.

"Am I furious with him? Because I will be. Just tell me. Furious or is this forgivable? I don't know so you'll have to be in charge of my emotions about it."

"You aren't furious."

"Good."

"You might be very very sad. You might be so sad you might

never recover. You might have a broken heart that is so shattered that you might wallow in misery for the rest of your days, but the one small shred of peace in it all — it wasn't his fault he left."

She put an arm around me and squeezed. "I feel a bit better knowing that."

The nurse entered and went over my list of things I needed to do, eat, drink while I recovered. She looked at Hayley the whole time like I wasn't even there. I was useless, incompetent, overwhelmed.

I climbed into a wheelchair and the orderly wheeled me to the front doors where Emma was waiting with her car.

They helped me into the front seat and then Hayley grumbled about having to sit in the backseat with Ben. "Seriously, Ben? There's drool all over your shirt. It's sopping wet. How are we going to take you anywhere?"

Ben giggled.

I said, "I don't want to go anywhere."

Emma said, "Well, there's not really anywhere to go. The house is packed up and Magnus said you shouldn't go there. The new apartment isn't set up yet."

My lower lip trembled. "I just need the bed. Can you ask them to get that moved in?"

"Sure Katie." She texted Zach.

I closed my eyes and waited.

She said, "Okay, they're moving your mattresses into your apartment now. He'll make sure the bedding is there too. Would you like some food on the way?"

"French fries."

"Perfect."

Trees slid by the window as we drove down 14th Street. "I'm really sorry we have to move, Emma. I'm sorry about the disruption. I hope you guys will forgive me for it."

She put her hand on mine. "Consider it forgiven. Besides, even this apartment is better than the other places I've lived. You know last time I had to move I had to borrow money for the deposit and my landlord was a total nightmare. Zach's last apartment was a dump. This is fine. Don't worry about it." She drove me toward my new empty home.

MAGNUS

$\mathcal{U}$nnnggghhhhh. Unnnggghhhhh. I pulled myself up through a tunnel of torment and forced my eyes open tae check on Kaitlyn. Was she all—

It hit me that she wasna here. Couldna be here. And I faded under the darkness again.

I woke with a start. My eyes were blinded by a bright, stark, painful light. A beeping sound so loud it hurt my ears. I was held tight — I pulled at my arms and legs and attempted tae turn my head. Twas nae possible tae move. I stared up at the ceiling attemptin' tae gain any information about this place. But twas only light and white. I closed my eyes against it and waited for somethin' tae change.

"Magnus Archibald Caehlin Campbell?" The voice was female and close tae my ear. It's closeness startled me. My first thought, *Kaitlyn?*

I couldna see who was addressin' me.

"Who?" My tongue felt thick from disuse. *How long had I been here?*

"Magnus, I'm Dr. Thompson."

"Where am I?"

Her voice seemed tae be disembodied. "You are in the Royal Infirmary. The year is 2381. You've been here for three days."

"Why?"

"It's standard after someone comes forward in time. A blood test has proven your genetic identity and you are of clean health. I've been given permission for you to enter the court as soon as you're ready to go."

"I canna move."

There was a soft clicking sound and it felt as if a blanket peeled from my skin. I sat up and swung my feet over the side of the stark flat bed.

The room spun. I collapsed back tae the bed again. "I canna sit up."

There was no answer. I turned my head tae look around the room squintin' tae see the forms, white and indiscernible in the glare of the lights. Twas like sittin' inside the sun.

I attempted a sitting position again and directed my focus.

My clothes were folded neatly on a metal table. They smelled foreign and laundered. My jaw was without its beard. My fingernails were clean. I dinna like the idea of bein' shaved and washed while unconscious.

And I dinna have my sword.

I stood in front of the door. Cast with light in front of me was my own image, much like a mirror. More light surrounded by light. I closed my eyes against the onslaught.

An opening appeared midway down. The voice from near my ear said, "Insert your wrists."

I placed my hands through the hole and a rope bound my wrists verra tightly. Twas metallic the same as the band Kaitlyn wore around her neck.

The door clicked and swung open.

The voice beside my ear said, "It was a pleasure meeting you, Magnus."

I stepped into a hallway. In the brightness I had difficulties seein' the way. I stumbled against a wall and recorrected blindly. After some distance I came tae a length of windows — I was inside a bridge of glass high above the ground connecting... I pressed to the window to see where the bridge originated — behind towered a building built mostly of glass, glintin' in the sun. Ahead of me stood a grand castle built of stone. Twas larger than I had ever seen. Below were lush gardens, a giant arena, a forest and mountains beyond.

Farther along, the windowed walkway ended and I entered the stone hallways of the castle. The stone provided some relief for my eyes.

I approached two men guardin' a double door. The doors swept open and I entered a grand hall that stored massive quantities of antiques and art. There was barely any room tae stand.

A different voice said, "You can wait here."

I stood in the middle of the room and took it all in.

The rooms of Lady Mairead in the eighteenth century had been full of plunder but this room held many times more. Art leaned against the walls ten paintings thick in places. Sculptures stood in most open areas leaving verra little walkin' space between them. Rolls of tapestries leaned in corners and stacks of china stood on ornately carved tables. The ceiling was an image that shifted and moved, illuminated — two men fightin' with swords in an arena.

I waited.

After standing shackled for a verra long time, the door at the far end of the room opened and Lady Mairead stepped through. Her hand was wrapped around the elbow of a man. She held a wide self-satisfied smile on her face.

He was the same as myself in look and stature, though his coloring was lighter. He wore a suit of a filmy, shifting material in a color like the wind. The shoulders and edges of his suit were trimmed in dark fur.

He and Lady Mairead stopped about ten feet away and appraised me.

She said, "Magnus, take a knee, tis your father."

I dinna want tae. I needed time tae decide before I bowed my head before this man, yet I dropped tae a knee.

He said, "He is much the way you described."

Lady Mairead said, "Larger even. He has been in training, as you requested."

"Perfect."

The man who was supposed tae be my father circled me. "You have done very well. He seems exactly as I asked."

My breaths were comin' fast. I asked, "Where am I?"

"You are in your court, Son, your kingdom. You are the heir to my throne."

I stared at his feet. "And who are ye? I daena believe we have met."

"I am Donnan the Second, born in the year 2330."

"And why have I never met ye before?"

He ignored my question. "Rise, I imagine you are hungry. We will go to dine."

The dining room was so large it overwhelmed the verra long

table. There was gold everywhere and porcelain, silver, and crystal place settings. Donnan took the chair at the head of the table. Lady Mairead sat tae his left. I sat on his right.

I glared across at Lady Mairead. She had assured me there was nae danger, yet here I sat, a prisoner.

"I winna be able tae eat without my hands."

"You will make do, I would think," said Lady Mairead.

Donnan said, "If you are as bloodthirsty and furious as Mairead promised, you would be a dangerous dinner guest without bindings."

The edge of his lips went up in a smile. "So tell me about yourself, Son."

"Am I allowed tae leave?"

His eyes leveled on my face while he spoke tae Lady Mairead. "He answers questions with questions?"

Lady Mairead demurely bowed her head. "Tis one of the things that makes him a good warrior, a willfulness that canna be broken."

He paused with his fingers itchin' beside the base of his knife.

My place settin' had nae knife.

He said, "My kingdom spreads throughout the hemisphere, Magnus, and you are next in line for the throne. You proved your lineage with the testing we did once you arrived. Next we will prove you are ruthless. This will be arduous yet necessary and until I can be assured of your cooperation, I can't let you roam freely. Surely you must see that. Also, there are a great many people who want to take your place."

A plate of food was placed in front of me. I was famished. I managed tae pick up the fork, stab the meat, and raise the whole cutlet tae my mouth. I gnawed on it.

Lady Mairead winced.

I chewed with my mouth open starin' at her forehead, darin'

her tae look. I swallowed and asked, "If I am your heir, why have I been livin' in the past?"

"Your great-great-grandfather, Aenghus III, killed his brothers to take the throne. Since then the line of succession hasn't been safe from those willing to fight for it. I was raised in the past myself until I was of age. For my own protection. Now that you're able to fight you can protect yourself."

I continued to chew and stare at Lady Mairead. "Who would I be protectin' myself from?"

"Your brothers. Your uncles. My brother, Tanrick, believes he should rule. My half-brother, Samuel. There are many others. I have followed your exploits. I believe you are ready."

I growled. "Ye mean ye have been playin' games with me, putting Kaitlyn in danger tae test me. Tell me Donnan, did ye order Lady Mairead tae hire criminals to steal Kaitlyn away?"

"You are confused, Son, to think you get to ask questions of me."

He took a bite of his meat, carving a piece, chewing with deliberate slowness. Then he said, "I might ask of you, how is it that Mairead has these scars upon her cheeks? I think you have not been able to protect her. I believe it is a recurring theme with you, promising protection and not delivering it."

My leg shook; I wanted tae charge him. He ate as if he had all the time in the world.

Donnan shrugged. "So I ordered some tasks for you, some incentives to help you train. You needed to learn to focus."

"Games," I slammed the fork tae my plate. "With my wife's life at risk."

"Hush Magnus," urged Lady Mairead, "watch your tongue".

"I will nae watch my tongue any more than I will remain here fightin' for a throne I daena want."

Donnan looked from my face tae Lady Mairead's. He seemed mildly amused.

She on the other hand looked furious. "Magnus, much trouble has gone intae getting ye here. Everything I have done is for you, tae prepare ye for this—"

I banged my fists on the table and stood leaning over it. "You have nae done one thing for me. Not one—"

She leveled her gaze. "I got you Kaitlyn."

"But you dinna let me stay with her!" The guards closed in behind me, four. Twould be difficult tae fight four without the use of my hands.

"Tsk tsk," said Donnan. "Is this all about the Kaitlyn Sheffield of yore? This is why you're angry, Magnus? Because Kaitlyn Sheffield is long gone, there's no sense in dwelling on the past."

I lunged aiming my bound hands at his throat. "Her name is Kaitlyn Campbell!" I was dragged off the table, draggin' a plate and a glass along tae crash tae the floor.

Donnan said, "Show him to his rooms."

I was dragged strugglin' tae the door by guards.

I managed tae knock a sculpture and then a table over with a crash of glass as they forced me down the room. I was shoved to the hallway, then forced tae stand and walk between the guards down another long stone passageway tae a far away door. I was shoved through.

The door closed shut and locked behind me.

An entirely new room — so bright I could only make out the larger details. I had tae keep closin' my eyes against the strain of it. There was a wall of windows looking out over a lush land-scape. I guessed I was about five stories above the ground. The gardens below had a maze, walkways and paths, and manicured grass stretchin' a fair distance. I could see the edge of the large arena that I noticed earlier from the bridge. There were mountains in the cloud-covered distance but I couldna make out the peaks.

Within the room against the wall stood a large, ornately carved bed covered in lavish bedding. On the floor was a woven rug.

In front of the far wall, a light-cast, an image — a Scottish landscape, a familiar landscape — highland stones and craggy rocks. It shifted as if twas alive.

There was a fireplace on the opposite wall, with a small crackling blaze on the hearth. The sound of it filled the room.

The only other furniture was a small table with two chairs and beside that, a doorway tae a closet. Another door opened tae reveal a modern bathroom: a shower, a toilet, a sink.

My wrists were still bound. I banged on the door with my fists. "You forgot tae take the shackles off!" The same kind of small opening slid wide. I put my fists through and the metal bindings peeled from my skin.

I rubbed my wrists trying to remove the feeling. *I remember... tis like a vibration on my skin.* Fury rose in my chest — fury at everything they had stolen — that they were stealin' from me.

The bathroom had a mirror and I checked around my neck. A square of metal much like a bandage was adhered behind my ear. It wouldna be easy tae escape with this magic on my skin.

The shower controls were confusin' and I dinna want tae think on it much so my shower was uncomfortably cold.

When I emerged from the bathroom, the wall of windows had turned dark. The gardens below twinkled with lights along the trails and paths. The sound of insects at twilight was amplified uncomfortably loud through the room.

The projected Scottish landscape dimmed as well. I had nae idea if it was truly night — what was real and what was bein' invented — it all felt much like imprisonment. I climbed intae the bed, pulled the covers up, and the last light in the room went thankfully dark.

My horse was at a full gallop. I held the reins tryin' tae keep her under control, my sights on the horse ahead of us, tearin' down the road. Kaitlyn was ridin' it, and the horse kept going. She was always ahead, never slowin' or faltering. Fear surged when I saw the horse near a tree, but it dodged without breakin' stride, and nae matter how I rode, how much I urged my horse, it wasna good enough. I couldna get tae her, fast enough — "Kaitlyn!"

I sat up gasping and clutched my chest tryin' tae get above the wave of fear takin' my air.

A woman's voice beside my ear asked, "Which Kaitlyn are you speaking of?"

I wasna keen on answering, so I ignored it, yet it pressed, "Which Kaitlyn?"

"My wife, Kaitlyn Campbell." I spoke it intae the dark air with my head bowed.

The light changed in my room and the far wall brightly glowed. I looked up tae see an image of Kaitlyn Campbell that took my breath away. It was large. I was drawn toward it as it shifted. She was lookin' down and then her eyes looked up, her face opened intae a smile. Someone or something caused her face tae light in happiness.

She was smilin', staring out at something I couldna see. I changed positions tae look her directly in the eye, but she continued tae stare above my head, beyond me, intae the distance. What was she smiling at? She looked older. Her hair was different. Who was she smiling toward?

I asked, "When was this?"

The voice answered, "This photo was taken on December 10, in Florida, the year 2028. Kaitlyn Sheffield Campbell was thirty-four years of age."

The photo shifted again, Kaitlyn, her face lighting up at the sight of someone.

"How long ago was this?"

"This was three hundred and fifty-three years ago. Would you care to see more?"

I sat down on the bed.

"Nae, tis enough. Keep it on."

I watched the image shift, Kaitlyn's face lightin' up. "Can ye tell me about her?"

"Kaitlyn Sheffield Campbell, born December 5, 1993, married to Magnus Archibald Caehlin Campbell," said the voice, "on July 2, 2017."

The voice continued, "Kaitlyn Sheffield Campbell lost her husband on October 24, 2018. She signed the Death in Absentia judgement and was declared a widow on November 29, 2028."

"So this image was taken soon after she became a widow?"

"Yes, eleven days later."

I watched the loop of Kaitlyn smilin' over and over.

"Would you like to hear more?" asked the voice near my ear.

I watched the shiftin' and the smile of my wife. "Aye."

"Kaitlyn Campbell gave birth to a son, Maddox Carter Wilson, born on April 25, 2029." The image shifted tae Kaitlyn, smilin' and holdin' a bairn in her arms.

"Och." I collapsed on the bed.

After a moment I managed tae ask, "Who was the father?"

The lightin' in the room shifted. I ken the photo had changed tae the man who fathered Kaitlyn's child but I couldna look.

"The father was Tyler Garrison Wilson, born January 9, 1992."

I asked, "Did they marry?"

"There are no records of a marriage between Kaitlyn Sheffield Campbell and Tyler Garrison Wilson."

I stared up at the ceiling. "Can ye tell me what happened tae her, how she ended?"

"Kaitlyn Sheffield Campbell died on July 2, 2076 at the age of 83. She was surrounded by friends. She was survived by her son, his wife, and two grandchildren. She was cremated."

I sat up and looked at the newest image — Kaitlyn, older. Her hair turned gray, her face lined. The smile though. The eyes. Twas Kaitlyn smiling through the years.

"Can ye remind me how long ago this was?"

"Kaitlyn Sheffield Campbell passed away three hundred and five years ago."

"I daena want tae see anymore."

The room returned tae darkness.

But when my eyes closed there was a glowin' shape, Kaitlyn, as if she was an echo inside me.

I pressed m'fists tae my eyes. "She is safe."

"Who is safe?" asked the voice.

I slammed my fists tae the mattress. "I daena want tae talk anymore."

"Yes, Magnus, good night."

I breathed in and out. "She is safe. She lived on. She had a child. She was happy."

I banged my fist on the mattress. "She lived a long life without me. She was safe and good and wasna that what I wanted? That was all I wanted." I yelled at the ceiling, "All I wanted was for Kaitlyn tae be safe. Without me she was. She had a child. Grandchildren. Without me she was."

She was.

She was the past, nae more than dust.

My voice cracked apart and turned tae a cry. "Without me she was." I hit the mattress. My fists were nae full of fury but of pain. I pulled tae my side and couldna understand how tae go on from here...

KAITLYN

I heard shattering glass and activity in my living room and then my bedroom door slammed open, but what was I going to do about it? If it was a thief, they could have it. All of it. I shimmied down into my covers.

The bed shifted like that one time months and months ago when Magnus came home. It wasn't Magnus though, not anymore.

Hayley's voice said, "Hey, sweetie, how ya doin'?"

I stared at the underside of my sheets.

"You doing okay?"

I burst into tears.

"Yeah honey, I know." She nudged me a bit, so I moved over and then she laid down on the bed beside me. "I know."

I cried for a long while. Not about anything in particular, not anymore, but about everything. Then I asked, "How'd you get in?"

"Quentin broke out a window. We are super worried about you and so you don't get a glass window anymore. You should have answered your phone."

I pulled a tissue from the box I kept under the sheets with me and blew my nose. "I don't really want to see anyone."

"Yep. We know. But sometimes you don't get what you want."

I sobbed. "I never get what I want."

"It kind of feels like that, huh?"

I nodded my head under the covers probably adding to the matted-hair thing I had going. It had been a while since I wasn't in bed. *How long?*

"What time is it? What day?"

"It's 10 am, Saturday, November 3. It's very dark in here. These are some excellent window coverings by the way. I need these in my house so I can sleep better."

She didn't say anything more and I didn't answer so we sat there in silence for a few moments.

I said, "You don't have to stay here. You checked on me. I'm sure you have something to do."

She huffed. "Well, see, that's not how this works. First, your house has a broken window out front so someone needs to stay here and deal with that. Second, while I have heard your voice now, so I don't have to think terrible things happened to you, past tense, I'm even more worried about what *might* happen. Because this doesn't look good. So I'm not leaving. I'll live here if I have to. Because you're a wreck. And rightly so, I get it. I understand. We all understand but it's time to let us help."

"I don't want any help. I just want Magnus to come home."

"Yeah, me too." She curled on her side facing me, a lump under the covers. "But he didn't sound like he was coming home, honey. Like he didn't know if he could. That's what you told me so I don't think you can keep going like this. It's not waiting, this is giving up. This is sad. This is dying inside, sweetie. Let us help you."

I stayed quiet because she made me cry again a little.

She kept talking. "Zach and Emma are really worried about you. Have you seen Ben?"

"No, I can't."

"But he's finally getting interesting — sadly no tattoos yet, but he's got a little swagger."

"You are a terrible aunt."

"Yeah..." she paused. "Zach said you've been ordering food from delivery places. You know he sees the delivery men at your door. You pay him. You pay him a lot of money. You should let him cook for you. You should let Emma clean up around here. You haven't even opened a box."

"Quentin and Zach moved it all in here and I... I hate it. This isn't my house. I don't want to live here."

"I know you know this already, but Zach's parents are pressuring him to face reality and get a 'real job.' Emma's parents hate him, and want her to move to Gainesville for 'stability.'"

"He has a real job. It's stable. For as long as—"

"You aren't throwing off a real stable vibe, sweetie. So he's getting a lot of pressure and he's going to have a conniption. He's going to throw himself in front of one of the food delivery cars and then that will be it for him. And then Emma will be right next door crying while you're crying and it will be all your fault—"

"I don't think you're helping."

"Exactly! But I want to. I just don't know what to do or say — what is a bestie supposed to say, 'I'm sorry the love of your life is gone?' It doesn't seem like enough. How am I supposed to help?"

"I don't know."

"See, and you know how to do everything."

"I don't know how to keep Magnus here."

"Well, Magnus is in many ways an impossibility. Some things can't be helped. Even you couldn't do it, and you were the head of our prom committee and really did that whole thing by yourself. Plus you went to prom, looked beautiful, and were the prom queen. So yeah. You can do anything but *this*. And this is big. Bigger than big. Your man crossed time for you and would do it again in a heartbeat if he could but..."

I pulled the covers tighter over my head. "I just want to be alone."

Hayley huffed. "I know you do but here's the thing — I can't leave."

I sighed and forced out, "Why not?"

"I'm... I'm kinda going through something. I don't know how to..." She sighed. "You know how Michael is in the classes? He's got two night classes now and one on Saturday and it's been really weird. I'm at home by myself. I've been drinking a lot and... I was thinking I don't really like how that's making me feel."

I pulled the covers down to see her face.

She continued, "Like I'm supposed to be the fabulous one, right? But I'm at home alone while he's bettering himself and the drinking — you know you might not have noticed but I've been doing that a lot and... I don't really know what to say about it. I'm just going through something and wanted you to know."

"Really?"

She huffed again. "I mean I'm not talking about going total transformation. I don't want to quit or anything but I just need something else to do. So that I'm not feeling like I'm useless."

I watched her face to know she was done, then I said, "I love you and I really wish I could throw the covers off and climb out of bed and be the kind of person who could make a list of fun things we could do while Michael is in class. But I have a giant gaping hole inside and all I can do is fill it with tears and then try to keep my head up so I don't drown. And I'm sorry that I can't be better. But I just can't."

She said quietly, "Sweetie, I'm not asking you to be that

person. I know you can't. I'm asking you to let me take care of you."

We both sat there for a little while.

Finally I asked, "What would that even mean, 'take care of me?' I mean, you want to make me food? Go grocery shopping?"

"Hell no. I mean, I would if that's what you wanted, but I could come help you unpack boxes. I could call Zach and tell him what to cook for you. I could go next door and pick up the food. I could give Emma a list of things to buy. I could do all of those things. We could watch movies and you might feel a little better and I might feel a bit of purpose and maybe we can help each other." She added, "While watching Paul Rudd."

"I don't like Paul Rudd anymore, maybe Chris or Liam Hemsworth."

"Yum. We can have a Hemsworth binge-watch."

It was my turn to sigh and I did it dramatically. "Okay, you can come over here. Please use a key, there's an extra in the drawer by the kitchen sink. You can unpack some boxes. But you have to ask me first. I do not want you putting up pictures. I'm not ready for that. But it would be nice to have my clothes unpacked. I've been wearing this for days and days and days."

I flounced to my side wrapping the covers all around me. "But I'm not getting out of bed. Maybe to go to the couch for a little while. But don't get all pushy. And I can't see Ben yet. I just can't. I just. Can't."

"Okay. I'll tell Emma. I love you. Thank you for letting me help. And speaking of wearing your clothes for days and days when was the last time you showered?"

"Hayley, don't get pushy."

"Fine."

MAGNUS

Four men crashed through the door tae my room and wordlessly grabbed me from bed, overpowered me when I struggled, and shoved me in front of Donnan.

"It's your first trials today, boy. You should rise."

"I am risen already, thanks." The light burst upon me so brutally fast my eyes watered.

"Don your kilt. You fight in a few minutes."

"Who? Why?"

"Your Uncle awaits. You stand between him and the throne. He wants to kill you before you take the throne. Your weapon of choice is a sword, I believe?"

"Aye."

"There will be a sword at the arena." He swept from the room.

I dressed in the bathroom. When I emerged the guards grabbed me by the arms, shoved me intae the hallway, and fell intae position around me forcin' me down the hall. We traveled down five floors in an elevator, along another long passageway that seemed tae go underground, and finally, I was pushed through tae a small room with double doors at the opposite end.

The voice that was missin' from my ear since I told it tae turn off last night said, "Magnus, get ready, the fight begins in three, two, one—"

The doors swung open ontae a cavernous arena, the biggest I had ever seen and I had tried tae watch a soccer game on the tv with Zach.

The arena was open. The sky was bright and blue. I was grateful tae see it after many long days. The walls were flat and vertical and covered with movin' images of people cheering and yelling and clapping. Tens of thousands of people. The sound pounded in my ears. A roar. Twas verra hard tae concentrate, but I had tae — a lone man stood at the far opposite end.

He was dark. We were similar in size and shape, fairly matched. He wore a helmet, a chest plate, and carried a sword.

He called across the way, "Suit up boy!"

To my right stood a sword, a helmet and a chest plate. I checked that he wasna movin' but he seemed ready tae watch as I dressed in the gear.

I picked up the sword. It had a good weight and heft, but as soon as it was in m'hand the man charged, yellin', his blade held high. The crowd was loud with cheering. He brought his sword down hard. I met it with my own swingin' up toward him, meeting blade tae blade.

He swung again knockin' my blade tae the side with the force of a seasoned fighter. "Ah, the usurper, come to take my crown? You fight like a child."

The audience laughed, some faces were enlarged, while others were small, movin' in and out, jeerin' and laughing.

I sliced my sword up through the air forcin' him tae take a step back.

I asked, "I daena believe we've met, who are ye?"

He spoke, loud and boisterously, as if performin' for the audience. "I am your Uncle Tanrick. The true heir to the throne yet all I do these days is fight the sons of Donnan."

I swung, meetin' his blade with a loud clang. "Now see, I daena want your throne, Uncle. So you and I, we can just lay these swords down and maybe have a beer together."

He thrust toward me his blade uncomfortably close tae my side.

I said, "I would much rather return home and ye could go about your business of fightin' the other sons." I lunged toward his arm. If I knocked his sword from his hand I might wrestle him down without killin' him.

Tanrick paused and smiled. "The only way I am laying down my weapon is beside your corpse, Nephew."

My breaths were fast. "Twas nae my intention tae be killed this morn." I swung my sword but he swung to meet it and caught me off guard using my balance against me. I stumbled back while he charged.

His blade sliced down and bit into my left shoulder. "Nor I, yet one of us must die."

I dropped to one knee with a groan. I used my sword tae lean on as I climbed tae my feet. "How many sons have ye fought?"

"I've killed three so far including you."

He seemed to be catchin' his breath so I took a moment tae size him up. He was comin' from the high right each time. I needed tae guard there and move to his left.

"You haena killed me yet."

"That's because I'm taking my time, making it pretty for the audience." He turned to the light-cast audience covering the walls around us. "Are you ready to see the son of Donnan die?"

The cheering was deafeningly loud.

He came at me with his sword swinging. I met it, blow for blow, our blades clanging and crashing against each other, gaining ground, then losin' it. Forward and back trying tae find the weakness in each other—

He lunged.

I dodged the blade but nae enough, blood flowed from a gash on my right shoulder. His smile turned malevolent.

"You are bleeding from both arms now, smile for the people of the kingdom, Nephew, they like to watch the royals die."

I leveled my gaze to his eyes. Focus, Magnus, focus. He means tae kill ye. Twould all be done then. I concentrated on his small shifts. He was tryin' tae confuse me. I saw in a glint, a vibration, he meant tae come from the left.

I raised my sword and charged his right. He raised his blade and as I sliced toward him I spun and arced slicing across his ribs. He clutched his side. It wasna a mortal wound, yet painful enough.

We both paused tae catch our breath. I was strainin' tae hold my sword.

He glanced down at the blood on his hand. "The people like a show, Nephew. You are weaker than the last though. He lasted twice as long before he had wounds like yours."

My fury rose, a wave of hatred engulfed my body and aimed for his smug face. He deserved tae die. He had been killin' my brothers, and meant tae kill me? Twas time for him tae go. "Thank ye for the vote of confidence. I wouldna count on being the victor though. I have come back from worse."

He lifted his sword and we prowled around each other, both lookin' for the weak spot, concentratin' while we recouped our strength. Readyin' for a final fatal blow. He lifted his sword and made the same move he had been makin', arced down from the right. I dove tae my right and thrust — a cut deep intae him in the abdomen under his ribs. I was roarin' at the time and shoved harder against him, my blade clean through until it wouldna continue.

His eyes met mine with so much hatred I couldna bear tae touch him anymore. I pushed him tae the ground and used my foot tae hold his body while I yanked my blade from him.

I looked around at the light-cast, shifting images of the roaring crowd. The sound was so loud I wanted tae drop my sword and cover my ears, but I dinna ken if the fight was over.

A man's voice from near my ear said, "Say your full name, Magnus."

"My name is Magnus Archibald Caelhin Campbell—"

"Louder, demand to be heard."

I yelled, "My name is Magnus Archibald Caehlin Campbell!"

The crowd erupted into a new explosion of applause and cheering.

The voice said, "You are the heir to the throne of Donnan. Say it."

"I am the heir tae the throne of Donnan!"

"Perfect." The image of the audience slowly faded around me until they disappeared altogether, taking the racket with them. It grew quiet and still in the arena, just the heat of the sun bearing down on me, my ragged breaths, and Tanrick's body at my feet.

I tossed my bloodied sword to the ground beside him.

MAGNUS

y wrists were bound. My hands were still bloody.
Blood had stopped flowin' from my shoulders but
it covered my clothes. I was ushered intae Donnan's grand sitting
room.

"Billiards, Magnus?" He stood beside a large table covered in
green. I guessed from the balls twas a game.

"I haena played before."

"I can teach you." He ran his hand along the felt on top of the
billiard table. "I got this from a brothel in 1845. If it could talk —
imagine the asses that have been planted here, right Son?"

I decided nae tae answer.

Donnan set a group of balls in the center of the table with
quite a bit of fussin'. Using a long stick he leaned over the table
and hit a ball — thwack. Balls spun away in all directions.

"Excellent job in your first trial by the way. Tanrick was a
particular pain in my ass. I decided not to kill him early on. I let
him arena fight but then the people loved him. I was having
trouble deciding what to do with him. Then he killed my first
two sons."

"How many sons dost ye have?"

"As many as it takes to secure a crown."

"Tis nae an answer."

"Yes, but it suffices because I say it does."

"I would battle better if I kent the battle was comin'. If I could prepare."

Donnan seemed tae have forgotten tae teach me tae play. Instead he made me stand and watch covered in blood and bound at the wrists.

"I'll set up some training sessions for you to keep you fight ready. You can go to the physician to see about your wounds. You'll take your meals in your room unless I send for you. Understood?"

"Nae."

"Nae? No? You don't understand?" He thwacked against the balls again sending three spinning toward pockets.

"I understand your instructions but daena ken the intent. I daena ken why I am held prisoner here. And I daena want the throne. There must be another son who wants the throne more than me, let him have it."

He smiled malevolently. "But the people already love you, Magnus, you can't turn your back on them now. Much like Tanrick, you have made yourself a warrior, but unlike Tanrick, you can actually rule once I pass you the throne." He strolled around the table. "But therein lies the issue. I am the ruler and I won't stand for a usurper taking it before I'm ready. You will remain bound so you won't kill me. I can see it in your eyes that you want to. Almost as much as you want to kill your dear mother. You are quite the son, Magnus, really."

He rolled a ball with his fingers. "I also have proof now from the arena that you could kill me if you wanted. So you'll stay a prisoner. But I also can't allow you to be killed by someone else."

He sat up on the billiard table. "I have many sons here as

well. They think they are capable, but they are soft and silly boys used to wealth. I have never intended for them to rule. They might wish you harm. So your rooms are guarded and only approved guests will be allowed in. That is the intent, to keep you alive so you may fight again."

I sighed deeply. "I will say it once more, I made a deal with Lady Mairead, I would come, I would fight for her tae gain what she wanted —"

"Queen Mother."

"Aye, she wants tae be Queen Mother, and I told her I would fight and—"

"For her to rise to the top of my women she must have a son that is prepared to become king. Else she is nothing to me."

"Tis nae concern of mine."

Donnan leaned on the edge of the billiard table and crossed his arms over his chest and made himself comfortable.

"What would you have me do?"

"Allow me tae return tae my home—"

"Scotland?"

"Nae, Florida."

"Ah, I see."

He sat for a long moment lookin' down at one of the billiard balls, twirlin' it in his hands. "You aren't thinking about this in the right way, Magnus."

"Thinkin' about what?"

"Your sweet Kaitlyn, living in an apartment she bought with your money, two hundred and some years ago."

"How dost ye know where—"

"There were a couple of years there that are murky, but as she gave up waiting for you she forgot to be cautious. Two years from when you left I have access to the full history of her, Magnus. She posted photos. Her address became public. Her bank records are all there. The birth certificate of her son. This is what you don't understand — I have access to all the facts of her life. And they don't include you. I may not be able to get to her just after you left, but I can go to Florida just after her son was born. I can visit her any time I want. But don't despair. I won't, because you will comply."

That growl rose from my chest again.

"And I have given you the same incredible gift. The ability to jump through time. Time doesn't matter to you. You have become a visitor, timeless. Eternal in a way."

"I daena ask for it."

"But yet you have used it. You've jumped from your time to her time. And now you want to live there."

"I do."

"But she is just someone stuck in time. She remains there, fixed. But you Magnus, you belong here, among those of us that can undo time. You can journey. You can go to new places, new times, and in doing so, unfettered, you can meet new women. Have new wives."

"I daena—"

He waved my protest away. "You're young. You obviously think this Kaitlyn Sheffield had merit of some kind that is impossible to see from three hundred years on. I'll give you that. I rather liked watching her story unfold and when you provided me with a grandson to further my bloodline..." He shifted. "But she is no more. I fancied myself in love with a woman once who lived in Spain, in 1421. But she was from the past and I was from the future. Our paths would only cross once and then no more. She's long gone."

He pointed tae his head. "You don't want to lose your mind over women who are long gone. And this Kaitlyn died over three hundred years ago—"

"I want one of the time-journey vessels."

A smile spread across his face. "You are such a barbarian,

Magnus. I keep telling Mairead, they aren't vessels, they are called the Tempus Omegas."

"Tis a stupid name, I still want one."

He laughed incredulously. "You've all but told me you intend to leave and you want me to give you the means to do so?"

"Aye. Because you ken I want it, and I will kill ye tae get tae it."

He laughed outright.

"You are an excellent, bloodthirsty, scheming son. It will be a pleasure to watch you perform."

I glared at him and took a deep breath.

"This brings up a point though." He gestured toward the guards and one stepped from the room.

Donnan went back to playing billiards sinkin' two balls intae the pockets. He remained quiet and I was too furious tae speak. My arms were sore from the cuts. The most painful, the right, started bleeding down my arm again. There was a pool of blood on his carpet.

"I am bleedin'. I need tae visit the physician."

Donnan ignored me. Soon the guard returned leading Lady Mairead. Her head was bowed, her face bruised with a black ring around an eye. She quietly said, "Hello Magnus, well fought today."

"Thank you, Lady Mairead, you are lookin' well."

Donnan said, "I'm missing one of the Tempus Omegas. I have been speaking to Mairead on the matter and she doesn't know where it's gone. I believe you were the one who had it last?" He leaned over the table and thwacked the white ball intae the last balls, sendin' two more intae the pockets.

I glanced at Lady Mairead. "I lost the vessel in Scotland when I jumped."

Donnan rose quickly, raised the stick back, and swung it hard before I could even react. The blow was aimed at the cut on my left shoulder. It knocked the air out of me and dropped me tae my knees.

"Get up boy."

I stood with a great deal of effort. Then I stared into the space right above his right arm, his swingin' arc. I watched that spot. Tryin' not tae squint, tryin' tae focus despite the brightness of the room. Lookin' for the pattern in his movements.

"What happened to my Tempus Omega?"

"I lost the vessel in Scotland."

The stick arced down hard on that same spot. I stumbled two steps and righted myself and stared at his shoulder, watchin' for the motion that would come. I stilled my mind and my body and waited.

He smiled and spoke verra smoothly. "I will ask you one more time. What happened to my Tempus Omega?"

"I lost it in—" The stick came down fast but I got my bound wrists up, grabbed it, and yanked hard pulling him off balance as he stumbled. I broke the stick into a jagged bludgeon and thrust forward with the shaft at his throat before the guards pulled me kickin' and strugglin' off him.

He straightened the front of his fancy coat. "Take him to the infirmary. I can see he's had enough."

KAITLYN

*A*s Hayley and I threaded our way through the restaurant to the table, I grabbed her arm and yanked her to a stop. "Hayley, who is that sitting beside Michael?"

"Some friend of Michael's. From school."

"Hayley—"

"It's not a set up. I promise. He's just a friend. He's new to Jax and had never been to Amelia before. We aren't setting you up. We know better. It's only been six months since Magnus left—"

"Five months and twenty-two days." I corrected, more out of habit than anything. Soon it would be the six month mark and then I would round up and down like everyone else I supposed.

She struggled out of her jacket, slung it over her arm, and blew the bangs off her forehead. She was irritated but then she softened and smiled. "I know it's not six months yet. And I'm really glad you came out with us. It's been a very long time."

"Yeah." I took in air to steady myself.

"No tricks. It's just a guy. Sit at the opposite end of the table and ignore him completely. Or talk to me. We'll pretend like we're out on the town by ourselves and just let Michael pay for our drinks." She sighed. "Who am I kidding, he's a student, he doesn't have any money."

"Good thing you're his sugar mama."

We arrived at the table. Hayley kissed Michael and sat down beside him and gestured toward the empty chair so I would be at the far end from the random dude they invited. I scowled because it was my first night out with Hayley and I didn't want strangers to ruin it. Especially if it was harder than I thought. It was already harder.

Michael leaned forward, completely oblivious to the drama unfolding. "Hey Katie, this is Tyler. He's from New York. He goes to school with me at JU."

"Cool. Nice to meet you, Tyler." He was ordinary looking, like just a guy, but tall and with a muscular build. His hair was cut very short as if there was a military thing happening. We did an awkward wave from the opposite ends of the table. Michael continued, "He's never been to the Island before." Tyler smiled.

I said, "Cool," and gave Hayley a look that said, 'You are not doing enough to keep me from an awkward conversation with a stranger.'

She changed the subject. "Did you order for me, Michael, or do I have to go to the bar like a chump?" She grinned.

"I didn't know what you wanted, but I'll go get it for you." He stood.

Hayley said, "I want a Margarita."

Tyler stood up. "What would you like to drink, Katie?"

I panicked and said, "Um, nothing. I mean..."

Hayley said, "That's okay Tyler, Michael knows what to order for Katie." Then she tried with eye-signals and head gestures to get Michael to know what I wanted, but he was completely clueless about the drama unfolding.

Tyler looked from one to the other.

I blurted out, "I'm married."

Tyler said, "Oh. I mean, yeah. You have a ring on. I was trying to be polite."

"Yeah, of course. I'm just trying to explain the reason we're all being so weird — I'm married. He's just um... missing and it's my first time out since he's been gone."

"Oh, how's he missing? Military?"

"No, um... he went missing in Scotland," I said like that explained it.

"Well, I was just offering to buy you a drink." He joked, "Is he a big guy?"

Michael said, "Huge. He could kick your ass in a second."

Hayley smacked Michael's arm. "But he won't because he's nice. Michael, get Katie a Margarita too. And pay attention better. Be better at this."

"Better at what?"

She rolled her eyes. "Just go get us the drinks."

She turned to me once they left. "Sorry about that, sweetie. I'm going to turn my back on him after this and you won't have to say anything but to me."

"You were talking about Magnus in the present tense..."

"Yeah, I guess I was. Not sure how to talk about him. He's always been coming home before."

"Yeah, he's always coming home. And also not coming home anymore." I swallowed against the rise of tears and my trembling chin. "How did I let you talk me into this?"

She gave me a sad smile. "Talk you into going out? I talked you into it precisely because you needed to be talked into it. It's not good for you to spend all that time alone in the apartment."

"I see people."

"You see Zach, Emma, Ben and Quentin. And you only see them because they make you see them. You only see me because I make you see me. You know it's true. And you know you should try to see people."

A drink was placed in front of me and I took a swig and picked up the dinner menu. I joked, "Oh Hayley, you are so needy. Why do I have to do everything for you?"

MAGNUS

*M*eals were passed through a slot in the door. The voices near my ear guided me.

My door opened the second day and I was told tae go down the elevator tae a ground floor trainin' hall. My trainer was a light-cast, extra-large on the wall. His giant head told me what tae lift and when tae run and how fast.

My arms were still sore from the cuts, but I was healin'.

I was in a routine, nae thinkin', just doin'.

I trained and ate and tried tae sleep though twas broken by dreams. Night after night — Kaitlyn on the beach and she canna see me. Kaitlyn on the horse and she canna hear me. And a new one, Kaitlyn above me, on me, sitting astride, weighing me down, yet when I try tae hold her tae keep her there, she was light and shadow and nothingness. I tried tae hold her down, but she was only wind.

I could feel her on me — heavy yet also gone.

Twas the way it all was now.

Heavy and gone.

I watched the light-cast of her that night. I lay on the bed with it glowing on the wall watching her smile up at someone else. Over and over and over.

The next day was more of the same.

I knew the routine was goin' tae kill me. Twould be the death of me tae nae do anythin' but be alone. But I was too dark in my soul tae think of a way out of it.

Short of killin' Donnan.

But I had tae make sure I could get away after the deed was done.

I needed a vessel.

I asked the voice beside my ear. "Where does Donnan keep the vessels?"

A woman's voice said, "I'm not sure what you mean?"

"The vessels, the Tempus Omegas, for traveling through time?"

I waited, but the voice went quiet.

"Can ye tell me where they are kept?"

"No."

KAITLYN

I pushed the door open to her small apartment. "Grandma?"

"Who is that?"

"It's me, Kaitlyn Camp — I mean Sheffield, Katie Sheffield. Your granddaughter." I dropped my keys in my purse and hung my bag over the rack near the front door. "I'm Paige and John's daughter, you know, your son, John Sheffield?"

I glanced around the room. It was dark, but usually was on Thursday mornings. I tried to get here before the staff so I could take her to breakfast.

She was still in bed as usual. I turned on lights and opened the blinds letting the bright Florida late March sun stream in. "Good morning!" I said as cheerily as possible though cheery had been kind of a long distant memory. I pulled her bedcovers off while she still looked up at me confused.

"Katie?"

"Yep, Katie. I'm here for our breakfast date in the dining room. Twice a week whether you want it or not. Today's

Thursday so here I am." I gave her my arm and helped hoist her from the bed.

"Where's Jack?"

I sighed. "Jack is in heaven now, you'll see him someday."

I walked her to the bathroom and helped her use the toilet. She was distracted for a moment with all the activity. But then she said, "Jack would be worried about him. He really liked him." I helped her get back on her feet and led her to the bathroom sink and squirted toothpaste on her brush. "Who Grandma?" I watched her brush her teeth and pulled a hairbrush from a drawer and ran it through her thin white hair.

"Magnus, dear. He's been gone for a long time." She squinted her eyes as if she was considering new information. Then shook her head of it.

I smiled, because if you want to feel better the first rule is: smile.

I smiled like a maniac as I led my grandma to the dining room like I was the cheeriest fucker in the world.

Hey guys, it's me, Katie Sheffield. Except I'm married now. And my husband is missing. You may have heard — the whole island is talking about it. He's rich and missing and now I live in an apartment and people whisper about me and I have to ignore it. My friends have to treat me like I'm a special case. They whisper about me too. Things like, what day is your day to check on her? And, did you check on her yesterday?

Kind of like me checking on my grandmother every other day.

Because you never knew what each new day would bring — what kind of mortal blow.

Everyone knew us in the dining room. Grandma chatted with a few other residents and I bantered with our regular waiter.

Then Grandma said, "You look like hell."

"Thanks Grandma." I chuckled. "And who am I?"

"You're apparently John's daughter, Katie, though she used to be a happy kid." She stirred cream into her coffee.

"Yeah, the world has kind of beaten down little ol' Katie and turned her into the haggard depressed woman you see before you. I haven't been sleeping well."

"Why not?"

"I have terrible dreams. About Magnus."

She said, "Magnus was like family to Jack and me."

"He is family, I married him."

"That's right. I remember now. And he's gone. That's why he doesn't come to see me anymore." She stared off into space.

I sighed. She was especially weird today, spacey yet thoughtful. Like her brain was remembering things but the strain of it was overloading her synapses. She was also frail almost like she was withering away. "I've been having this recurring dream, I'm somewhere, like the beach—"

"Looking for shark teeth, you do love doing that."

"Exactly!" I beamed at her. She remembered something about me. "It's true, I love it. In my dream I'm looking down, but I can hear him — Magnus. He's yelling my name and I know he's nearby but I can't look. My head won't turn. It's like I'm purposefully ignoring him but I get frantic because I'm stuck, and—"

Grandma was looking right at me now listening and focused. "Are there more, dear?"

"Yes, in another one I'm looking up at this tree I saw once in Scotland. Magnus and I were arguing, but for some reason I noticed it. It was beautiful, two trunks entwined, and I'm looking up at the tree and I can hear Magnus calling me again. But I won't look away from the tree." The waitress poured more coffee in my cup and told us the food would be out in just a minute.

I finished, "There are more, but that's the crux, I hear him but I can't notice him. I guess it's just that he's missing... It's making my mind believe I can hear him."

"Oh it's much deeper than that, dear." Our plates were delivered interrupting her thought. We were offered ketchup, Grandma needed salt. She asked for more coffee. By the time the food was fully served I was pretty sure she wouldn't remember the conversation. But I was curious. I missed her helpful wisdoms so much.

"What were you going to say? You said, 'It's much deeper than that,' about my dreams — I'm sorry to press but ever since I lost the baby and then Magnus, I just need some advice."

She furrowed her brow for a moment then said out of nowhere, "Quantum entanglements, Jack is fascinated by them."

"I know the word, not sure I get..."

"Some particles become so close they can't be independent. Even when they're separated by a large distance."

I continued to chew a piece of bacon trying to grasp where her Alzheimer's-riddled mind was going with this.

But she seemed pleased with herself like that explained what she meant.

I asked, "What?"

"Dear, you were going to have his baby — did you know when you make a baby together, bits of the baby's genetic material become a part of your body? And the baby was made up of both of you so you are carrying bits of your baby and your husband inside — wrapped, tied, knotted — it's science."

"Really?"

"Yes, and if you're truly entangled, you would be tied even though you're separated by time and space. Hence the dreams."

"So you think Magnus is communicating through my dreams? It's not just my mind but it's really him I'm hearing?"

"No, that would be crazy. Maybe it's not crazy at all. Maybe what your dreams are telling you is don't give up hope, but to listen. To open yourself to the possibility you might be entangled with him still even though he's gone."

I looked down at my plate trying to think about all of that.

"Most of the time when I bring up Jack, you remind me that Jack isn't here anymore. And I know Jack isn't here. I know it here," she tapped on her temple, "most days. But here," she patted her heart, "he's still with me. I swear I can hear him sometimes. His shifts and movements, like he's just behind me. That's because I've got his genetic material tied to mine. It's overriding my common sense. He's present and he's everywhere, because he's in my particles."

"So I'm alive and it keeps Magnus alive?"

"Exactly."

I shoved my chair back, circled the table, threw my arms around my grandma, and held on.

MAGNUS

A few weeks later I was in bed when the guards barged intae my room and wrestled me tae standin'. I was told, "Dress, you'll be fighting this morning."

I yanked my arms from their grasp, got dressed, and fell intae line within their ranks down the long passage to the ground floor.

I was left in the stagin' room again staring at the door. My mind was full of fury. I dinna ken who was on the other side of the door, but I wanted tae kill him. Fast.

I had also done some thinkin' on the matter. My life was worth next tae nothin, but if the crowds liked me, I might gain a bit of power. Enough tae bargain with.

I asked, "Who am I fightin'?"

The voice in my ear said, "A brother, three, two, one, and go." The doors flung open on the projected crowds, their deafening cheers, a cloud-covered grey sky, and my opponent.

The man at the other end of the floor was big. Dark. He looked verra much like he wanted tae kill me. Twas nae a bit of charm in him, like facin' a bull, he pawed at the ground. I backed tae the wall for the large axe leanin' there. Not my favorite weapon — too top heavy, not weighted well, and for fightin' there wasna much forgiveness in it.

I grasped it while keeping my eyes on the man at the opposite end of the floor. "Hullo!" I called, "Are you my brother then?"

The man tossed his axe from hand tae hand and glared.

I tossed my axe and almost dropped it. I was watchin' my adversary and had forgotten tae consider the heft of it. The audience laughed.

"My apologies, Brother, I almost dropped m'axe. Would have made for a short fight I suspect." I had tae project my voice because he was such a great distance away.

"What's your name, Brother?" I spun the axe handle getting a feel for it in my palm, findin' the perfect balance.

The man across the arena grunted.

"I am Magnus Archibald—" The crowd chanted my name in unison and finished without my needin' tae. "...Archibald Caehlin Campbell!"

I chuckled, "I am the son of Donnan and next in line for the throne."

The man yelled and charged toward me with frightening speed. A few steps away he raised the axe over his shoulder and brought it down in a wide swing. I ducked and shuffled a few steps away. He narrowly missed, but I had risked it tae see his swing.

I tossed the axe tae my left hand and while he recovered from his swing, I swung. My axe arced up and caught his chest. Then I tossed the axe to my right hand and swung around hitting his left arm. My axe clipped his forearm causing a burst of blood.

My brother stepped back holding his cut and breathin' heavy. Hatred burned in his eyes.

"I want tae make ye an offer, Brother. The same offer I gave my uncle, Tanrick, just before I killed him a few weeks ago. If ye will lay down your weapon, we can come tae a place of peace." I was walkin' around him in a circle, lookin' for his weakness — his swing was comin' from the right after a short step for balance. I had injured him, but his swing would remain strong. It was at the downward turn where I would have him.

He shook his body getting the strength back tae his limbs.

"I have nae quarrel with you, Brother. I have been imprisoned the same as ye. Donnan is the one we should quarrel with."

He charged me and brought the axe down hard. At the bottom he took the extra step, momentarily off balance. He wasna as surefooted as before. I swung, hooked the end of my axe against his, yanked it from his grip, and flung it away across the floor. He recovered his feet and lunged at my chest too fast for me tae swing before the full weight of him was on me.

I was forced tae the ground. My axe flew from my hands. The audience gasped and grew silent.

He was on top of me raining down blows. I blocked, left, right, twistin' tae keep them from hittin' their mark. Then I used a move I had been taught in my trainin' in Florida. I wrapped my leg around his, grabbed him in a back hold, pulled him close tae my chest, and exploded up and over so I was on top of him.

Before he knew what was happening I was beatin' his face. Verra soon he was weak, bleedin', and barely fightin' back. I shoved off him and stood over him. "You had enough, Brother? Are ye ready tae submit tae me?"

He growled low and fierce and lumbered tae his feet. He charged me but instead veered and dove for his axe. I picked mine up. He was winded and slow. We eyed each other. I was regrettin' that I dinna finish him.

I wouldna make the mistake again.

He charged me, his axe raised, ready tae swing it down. I stepped back allowing it tae swing past me. Then when he was at the bottom of the arc, I leapt forward and swung across his middle, cutting a clean slice near through.

His axe fell and he slumped to the ground at my feet.

I stared down at him while the chantin' started. "Magnus, Magnus, Magnus!"

The voice in my ear said, "Your name is Magnus Archibald Caehlin Campbell..."

"My name is Magnus Archibald Caehlin Campbell."

"And you are heir to the throne of Donnan."

"I am heir tae the throne of Donnan."

"Louder."

"I am heir tae the throne of Donnan!"

The chantin' of my name was so loud I had tae clamp the heel of my hands over my ears.

But then the images of the crowd faded. The sound faded away until there was nothing but the grey sky above and yet another dead man at my feet.

The doors swung open at the end of the arena so I left.

I wasna invited tae see Donnan this time, and I dinna need the infirmary, so I was led by guards tae my room and left inside the door.

Kaitlyn was driving the Mustang. The roof was down. She was speeding. The music was loud and she was singin' and I was right there beside her — close enough tae hold her hand. But I was unable tae move, stuck, watchin' her sing and drive. I tried tae move tae touch her, tae see if she was real but I couldna move tae get close tae her...

KAITLYN

Quentin texted: Hayley is on the way up.

There was a knock on my door.

"Go away, I don't want to see anyone."

Hayley's voice carried through the door. "We already established that I'm an asshole who doesn't care what you want. You have to see me anyway, it's in the 'New Rules.'"

I was on my couch, shades drawn, ac full blast, watching Grey's Anatomy and eating from a box of chocolate chip cookies. I glanced up at the piece of paper Hayley had stuck with a magnet to my fridge. It was headlined, 'New Rules.' Number one was 'No one cares what you want, you have to see us anyway.'

Number two was, 'You have to see someone every day. Or we break a window.'

Number three was, 'Go see your grandmother at least every other day.'

Number four was, 'Zach gets to cook for you every day or he'll stop cashing his paychecks and Ben will starve.'

And so on for at least fifteen rules.

I called, "But today is an anniversary so the rules don't apply."

"No," came Hayley's voice, "that's not true. The rules on anniversary days are not voided they are doubled. You have to see me, let me in."

I said, "Fine," in the most irritated voice I could muster and went and yanked the lock. Then I slammed the door open, up against the wall, huffed at her, and returned to the couch. "What do you want?" I stared at the Grey's Anatomy episode again.

"Nothing." She sat down beside me without closing the front door and started texting. I watched her peripherally and a moment later Emma and Zach came in through the front door.

I pulled my phone up and texted while saying what I was texting, "Quentin, you didn't tell me I had these visitors. Worst security ever. You're fired."

He texted me back: Ha ha, nice try. I work for Magnus, you're stuck with me.

Everyone sat down around me on couches and chairs, just looking at me, expectantly.

"Hey everyone, to what do I owe this pleasure?"

Hayley said, "As you know, and we know you know because you're kind of being a bitch, it's your anniversary today."

I nodded, all their eyes on me. "I know."

Hayley added, "You've been doing so well. I haven't had to break out the 'New Rules' in months. I've been super proud of you, but I had a feeling today would be really hard so here we are."

"I see that. You're all here except Ben? He was too busy I suppose?"

Emma said, "Ben is taking a nap in our apartment. I have a monitor hooked up to my phone." She waved her phone towards me so I could see Ben sleeping.

"Great, he's the only one I really wanted to see." I smiled a little. They were already lifting my mood, but I didn't want to admit it.

Hayley said, "So Emma and I were talking about it the other day and we know what the problem is..."

"You guys were talking behind my back?"

"Jesus Christ, Katie, you've been the saddest case in the world for nine months. All we do is talk about you. When you go back to being a functioning human we'll stop, I promise."

"It's my anniversary and..."

"Yeah, there's a lot to get used to. But this is what we're thinking, you're ignoring your marriage to Magnus. It's like you're empty. You won't talk about him, you aren't reminding yourself about how happy he made you. You're wallowing in what's missing instead of remembering what you had with him."

Emma said, "We don't blame you, you lost the baby, you had to move, everything is boxed up, but we really think it's time to remember Magnus. It's your wedding anniversary and we're all here to help you do it."

My eyes flooded with tears. "It already sounds really painful."

Zach said, "Yep, that's why we're all here. And then we're going to have a little feast in his honor."

There was a knock on the front door. I yelled, "Come in!"

Quentin stuck his head in. "Katie, that is not how security works. Try again." He closed the door and knocked.

"Anyone but Quentin can come in!" I yelled chuckling to myself.

Quentin came in with a stern glare. "I have one job and you do not make it easy." He was carrying a box. He put it down in the middle of the room, went and locked my front door, and perched on the arm of the couch.

"What's this?"

Hayley opened the flaps of the box. "First, we're going to look at the photo and we're going to admire it and then I was thinking we could hang it." She pulled out the wedding photo of me and Magnus, the one where we were leaned back in our chairs after the feast. I had pulled it from the frame and given it to Magnus when he went to the past, but here it was, printed and in the frame again. It was passed through Zach, Quentin, and then to me. "You framed it for me again?"

"Emma did."

"Thank you."

"Remember when we took that? How scared you were?"

"I was. I was so scared. I married him without knowing anything about him."

Emma said, "But you were also having fun together and laughing. I remember thinking you were going to be really happy together because it was so easy between you."

I hugged the frame to my chest. "Okay."

Hayley said, "Okay, we can hang it?"

"Sure, yeah, okay." Tears streamed down my face. Zach went to the kitchen and pulled a hammer and a box of nails from under the sink. Everyone discussed where it should go and I didn't have an opinion so they chose the empty wall at the end of the living room. The photo was small for the space but that was okay.

Hayley said, "Okay, next."

She pulled out a box. It was clear glass soldered on the edges with a gold clasp. It looked beautiful and special. Inside was the red envelope with the letter from Magnus that he sent me through time. She passed it to Emma and she handed it to me. "Oh."

"Yeah, oh. I found that letter at the bottom of a cardboard box. You are the only person in the history of the world to have a letter passed to them through time by their three hundred-year-old lover. It belongs somewhere special."

I sniffled and put the box on the coffee table.

"Is that it? That's probably enough, right? I don't know if..."

Hayley said, "We have two more things."

She pulled a frame I had never seen before from the box. She held it for a moment and said, "Emma found the photo on your iCloud account. Don't be mad at her. Promise."

I squinted my eyes. I hated promising before I knew what it was. But I had never been mad at Emma before so I couldn't imagine what would make me start. "I promise."

She turned it around and I inhaled, a staggering inhale that caught twice in my chest. "Oh no."

"I know it's hard to look at, but we put it in this pretty frame and you can look at it in pieces, and then put it in a drawer. We just thought you would..."

I clutched it to my belly and looked down on it, the photo of Magnus kissing me while we smiled up, happy tears sparkling in our eyes. The morning we felt the baby move. The morning before I lost the baby. The morning before Magnus was gone forever. "If I only had a time machine to go back to that morning. I would tell myself to hold on to him harder."

I clutched it to my chest. "You said there was one more thing, I don't know if I can take any more."

Emma said, "This one is maybe the most poignant of them all, but also it's different. It was Zach's idea."

Zach said, "I was thinking that soon. Not today. Maybe not even this year, but sometime, you would want to go to Scotland." He was nervous and rubbed his hands up and down on his thighs sticking out at long angles from the chair. "That you would want to maybe look up Magnus's history."

My brow furrowed. "Like how he died?"

"I don't even know if that information would be there, but we could go look. Maybe you'd have answers. I mean, we'd all have answers. I wonder about him, and I tried to Google it and..."

"We?"

"Yeah, we'd all go with you. We'd help you look."

"We'd all go?" I was beginning to wonder if the tears would ever stop streaming from my eyes.

"Yes, all you have to do is ask and we'll all go."

Hayley pulled a stack of passports from the box and fanned them out. "Emma got all of our passports. You decide when you're ready to go, but when you are, we'll all get on the plane with you."

"To Scotland, to see where Magnus..."

Hayley said, "Exactly, to see where Magnus..."

I was still clutching that frame and didn't think I could let it go. "Okay. Thank you."

I stared at the new photo while my four friends sat awkwardly looking at each other and me occasionally and away, mostly.

Then Zach said, "Phew, that was one of the hardest fucking things in the world. Now we need some alcohol and food pronto." He stood and stretched. "Emma and I are hosting at our place."

Quentin joked, "But your apartment isn't as big." Quentin, Zach and Emma all stood up to go, talking and joking.

Zach said, "It's the exact same size. It's a mirror image of this place."

Hayley joked as they left, "It probably feels so small because there's a baby screaming his head off in there all the time. Tell Ben to get his emotions under control, pronto. People are calling him a big baby."

Zach said, "Yeah, yeah, see you in a few minutes, we have the alcohol."

They left and Hayley came over and sat with me on the couch. I leaned my head on her shoulder. She leaned her cheek to my head. We sat quietly for a moment. She asked, "Did we do good?"

"Yeah, you did good. I might never ever ever forgive you, but you did good."

MAGNUS

*T*was evening when the door tae my room opened. I rose from the bed but the guards dinna enter, instead they pushed a woman in and then left, closin' the door behind them.

I sat staring at her.

She leveled her gaze at me.

After a moment I asked, "Who are ye?"

"Donnan sent me. I'm a gift for you."

"A gift for..." I crossed the room and banged on the door. "Donnan! Guards! Bring the guards back!" I had yelled in the past though and no one ever came, just my voice echoin' through the hallways of the castle.

I turned back tae the room and the strange woman inside it. She was verra beautiful and had nae enough clothes on. Simply a wee cloth across her breasts and at her hips. I cleared my throat. "You arna welcome. I daena want a gift."

She said, "I volunteered. I'm Donnan's favorite and yet, when I saw you... I wanted to be yours. Now I'm here. I can't leave. I'm not allowed to. I'm a gift."

I took a deep breath. "I have nae need for a woman in my—"

She came close tae me and pressed against my chest. I stepped back. She followed me and pressed against my chest even more.

I pulled her hands off and pushed her back a step. "I have nae need for ye—"

She pointed at the spot behind my ear, the place where the metal patch was adhered tae my skin. She leaned forward and pushed the dark hair from her shoulder exposing the patch on the back of her own neck. She shook her head and repeated, "I'm a gift for you."

She nodded her head lookin' intae my eyes. "I can't leave. I'm not allowed to." She nodded again. She stroked down the side of my neck. "When presented with a gift like me, what do you say, Magnus? Would it be thank you? Would you welcome me?"

She nodded, but all the while lookin' in my eyes, beseechin' me tae understand. I said, "Aye, thank ye."

She nodded and smiled. "Would you thank Donnan for providing you with his favorite mistress?" She nodded more.

"Thank ye, Donnan, for the gift."

She ran her hands over my chest, spreading the folds of fabric. "Perfect. Thank you for the welcome. We're going to have fun." The words echoed in my head, remindin' me of Kaitlyn sayin', "*Want to do something fun?*"

She led me by the hand tae the bed and crawled intae it. I faltered standin' beside it. She put a finger to her lips tae tell me tae be quiet and mouthed the words, *trust me*. She patted the bed beside her, giving me space tae lay down without crowdin' me.

I asked, "What is your name?"

"My name is Bella."

I climbed in and she pulled the covers tae my chest and patted it. Then she curled up on her side and grew quiet. Nae touchin' just going tae sleep.

It was verra hard for me tae do the same with a beautiful woman in my bed.

~

I had my face buried in Kaitlyn's hospital gown. I was cryin' intae the folds. Her belly was soft with emptiness instead of full and round, and I was pulling the cloth tae m'face and tellin' her twould be okay and burrowin' deeper intae the cloth and then the cloth was empty, was nothin' but folds of fabric and loss and I couldna release my hands from it, couldna move—

Air rushed intae my lungs. I woke sittin' up in bed clutchin' the covers.

The woman — *what was her name, Bella?* — asked, "My Magnus, are you okay?" with a familiarity that made me want tae grab her by the arm and shove her through the door tae the hall, but I couldna because there wasna a way tae unlock the door.

I was a prisoner. She was a prisoner. Someone was listenin' tae us. Watching us. Lockin' us together when I only wanted tae be alone.

"Nae." I swung my legs tae the floor and stormed intae the bathroom tae shower.

~

The rest of the day was uncomfortable. The woman who lived here now got our meals when they were passed through the door and set them on the table and talked of inane things I dinna want tae talk of.

And as the day wore on her familiarity became more irritatin' tae my mood.

She kept the lighted images projectin' along the walls going with news stories. Twas too loud, images of explosions and war and — "Turn it off. I canna watch it. Tis too loud."

She asked the room tae turn down the volume.

I said, "The pictures are too loud as well."

"Oh, My Magnus, pictures can't be loud!" She laughed and asked the room tae turn the volume back up. "You are the son of the king. You have to know what is happening in the world." I watched the light-cast, bairn cryin' in a street of rubble. She watched my face. "Now that we live here together, I should teach you as much as I can about the world."

I stood and went tae the bathroom and stayed there prayin' on my knees, asking for guidance, until the voice in my ear reminded me twas time tae head tae the ground floor and the trainin' hall.

When I returned tae my apartments later I was resigned —Bella was a fellow prisoner and acceptin' her presence was the first step in figurin' out how tae survive.

The problem though with fellow prisoners is they want tae survive too and that made them dangerous.

I would need tae keep on my guard. "I want ye tae turn off the images. I canna think with it blarin' in the room."

"Yes, My Magnus." She was sprawled on my bed wrapped in the bedding with one of her legs exposed from the waist down.

I sat down on one of the chairs. "Where are you from?"

"From Spain. I came here when I was eighteen. I'm twenty-nine now."

"Och, and when — what year?"

She leaned up on an arm. "You don't believe I'm a woman from here, now?"

"I haena any idea. I haena met any women from this time. But Donnan is a collector. If he can bring sons from the past, I'm certain he brings women too."

She smiled. "You are correct. I came from 1640. It was quite a shock when I arrived. But I was trained in the arts of speech and beauty so I wouldn't be quite so uncivilized." She laid back on the bed, raised one beautiful leg up in the air, pointed her toes tae the sky, and then brought it down daintily.

I looked away.

She watched my face while I tried tae think of my next question. "Where are we?"

"Donnan's country estate."

"I meant the place name — the region or the name of the country, anythin'."

"I'm not allowed to tell you."

I sighed. "Can ye tell me, the mountains, what direction are they are in?"

"West, but you—"

"Where does Donnan keep the vessels, I mean the Tempus Omegas?"

"I don't know. And I wouldn't be able to tell you anyway. I'm not allowed to tell you anything." She sighed. "But you need to forget about returning to the past and live here and make the best of it."

Kaitlyn's words, *Begin where we are,* ran through my head. She would be devastated if she kent this woman was in my bed—

Bella noticed I scowled. "What are you thinking of, My Magnus?"

I put my elbows on my knees and watched her. "My wife, the one I left." It hurt tae say it that way, but twas also true.

"You regret leaving her? To come here and take your throne?"

She stretched long, her arms over her head, makin' herself verra desirable. She was beautiful, dark long hair, brown skin. She was well-curved and had a nice smile. "You get to live with me. Did your wife look like me?"

"Nae, she is taller in stature than ye. Her eyes are green and her hair a bit like yours, long, but of a different color. A chestnut, like a horse I once..."

"My Magnus, are you describing your wife like a horse?"

I shook my head. *Magnus are you comparing me to a horse?* "I dinna mean tae, but I canna think of another way tae describe it. It had a touch of sunshine on it. Golden in the light. Have ye ever seen eyes like — her eyes, when she smiled, looked like sunsets — have ye ever seen that? A smile that fills the eyes and draws ye in tae the horizon?" I finished, "She was verra beautiful. I spend a great deal of time thinkin' on her."

She sadly said, "My Magnus are you saying I'm not as beautiful as the wife you left?"

"I'm simply telling ye of her. Nae comparin'."

"Would you like to show me a picture?"

"Nae, I canna — nae."

"It is good though, you're speaking of her in the past tense. You left her. You're here with me now. This is the present. Being here with me in the present doesn't change how you felt about her in the past. They are two very different times."

I turned my ring around and around on my finger.

"One last thing. I heard another of Donnan's sons is here. I wanted you to know so you would be ready."

"You think twill be tomorrow?" I rubbed m'shoulder. It had been sore during the trainin'.

"It could be. If you're injured during the battle—" She seemed tae struggle with finding the right words. "If you're injured..." She looked intae my eyes noddin' slowly. "Don't argue, let them take you to the infirmary. Okay?" She crawled across the bed then rose tae her feet and came tae my chair.

She trailed a finger across my chest and prowled around draggin' it along my shoulders as she walked. She paused behind me and tugged on the back of my shirt. Her finger rubbed along one of my scars. "You have many scars here, My Magnus," she whispered. "What happened to you?"

"I was flogged." I pulled my shirt back tae rights.

"That must have been terrible. Who did it?" Her finger trailed as she came back to stand in front of me.

"Lady Mairead's husband, Lord Delapointe."

"Ah, you must be furious with her, that's good." She tucked a bit of hair behind my ear and seemed to change the subject. "I don't know what will happen to me if you don't survive, so go to the infirmary."

I furrowed my brow.

She said, "Promise."

"I daena like hospitals but I will go."

"Good, that's excellent." She kissed me on the forehead then she returned tae the bed, climbed on it, and rolled up in the bedding. She was sprawled across all the pillows starin' at the ceiling. "One more thing, My Magnus, make sure you tell everyone that you live with Bella now. Will you remember that?"

I watched her across the room. "What?"

"Say, to everyone, if they ask, that you live with Bella now. Just do."

I said, "Fine, if I get injured I will go tae the infirmary. If I'm in the infirmary, I will tell them that I live with you."

"Bella."

"I live with Bella."

She patted the bed beside her. "Want to come lie down, My Magnus?"

"Nae."

"Okay, suit yourself."

She continued runnin' her fingers along the wrinkles of the fabric staring at it as if she was used to being imprisoned, wastin' time, doin' nothing.

MAGNUS

I finally laid down when I got too tired tae sit in the chair anymore. Bella kept tae herself again, a wide space down the middle of the bed, so it wasna the physical famil-iarity that was botherin' me. It was that she was a part of my life, my house, and bed without any decision about it. I wasna settled with it.

I was thinkin' on it when the guards burst in the door with Donnan behind them. Bella put her hand on my chest.

Donnan said, "I can see you've been enjoying my gift, Magnus. Bella is a wonder isn't she?" His eyes had a look of violence that he tried tae mask with charm. I vowed right then I would kill him. Soon.

I got up from the bed and stretched out my right arm. My shoulder was verra sore.

"You have an injury, Son?"

"Nae, will be all right."

"Good, because you fight today. Another son has arrived. He awaits in the arena."

"I would be better able tae win if ye told me when I was expected tae fight. The surprise daena help my focus."

"What makes you think I want you to win?" He swept from the room.

I glanced over at Bella. She was uncovered naked on the bed. I shook my head of the sight of it.

She said, "My Magnus, don't forget to go to the infirmary when you're injured."

MAGNUS

A man's voice said, "Three, two, one, you fight, now," and the blindin' light of the overhead sun and deafenin' noise of the crowd hit me like from a cannon.

At the far end of the floor was another man if I could call him that — he was younger than me by a couple of years. He looked strong and ready tae fight but nae battle ready. I couldna believe he would be ready tae die.

The audience was cheerin' me, "Magnus, Magnus, Magnus!"

The man I was to fight shifted from one foot tae the other — light on his feet, excited, rarin' tae go.

"I am Magnus Archibald Caehlin Campbell." The crowd yelled my name in unison with me. I reminded myself tae smile, tae look as if I was comfortable here starin' at a stranger I needed tae kill.

A large hammer awaited me against the wall. I yelled, "Brother, I have nae quarrel with ye, drop your weapon. We can stand together."

"No, I think I prefer my odds in killing you."

"Great! We should get along terribly then." The crowd laughed.

I lifted the hammer. The weight of it was unwieldy. I swung and it changed direction — instead of arcin' gracefully the head dipped lower than I expected. "Did ye pick these weapons because they suit ye, or because ye dinna ken they are useless for battle. A hammer such as this is only good for forming metal."

I swung it again, whizzing it from left tae right. Its weight was already causin' a sharp pain in my shoulder. I massaged the tender spot near the front. There had been too much fightin' not enough living.

My brother called back. "I have been watching your fights. I sensed the hammer might be trouble for you so I've been training with it." He spun the handle of the hammer in his hands eyein' me the whole time.

"Ye ken a great deal more of me than I of you." I spun the hammer trying to get used tae the feel. "What is your name?"

"You'll know it when they're chanting it as you die at my feet like a dog."

I chuckled, more for the theater of it than for the humor. "You must come from a terrible place that dogs die at your feet. I prefer a place where dogs sit beside their masters and receive treats from the table. Want tae join me, Brother? I could offer ye a place in my court. Put aside our differences and—"

"I would rather die."

"If ye prefer it."

He charged toward me with his hammer raised. I swung mine in one hand and stepped forward tae meet him as he arced his towards my middle. Two steps and I hit him on the hip, stumblin' him tae the side. I missed. I was aimin' for his waist. He recovered easily.

We circled each other for a few steps. I thought I saw a ripple of movement from my left eye, so I swung but from the wrong direction. I was off balance when his hammer caught my side, knocking my breath from my chest. I stumbled three steps and was bent over when the hammer swung from my left and slammed into my sore shoulder knockin' me the other way. I was bent over and badly injured.

I tightened my hold on the handle, straightened with a groan, and stepped back.

I tried tae catch my breath. His eyes were focused, sharp, and hungry for blood. I hadna time yet tae see his swing and was too winded already tae take more blows.

I got into a defensive position, holdin' my hammer, nae smiling anymore. Twas nae time, he raised and swung.

I tried tae jump but miscalculated the speed of his swing. It hit me full in the ribs. The pain was blindin' — a*nd you have been whipped. Aye, I have been whipped* — my vision blurred. The glow of the lights and the pain in my ribs and the loss of air, made me — get tae your feet, Magnus, he will kill ye.

I forced my eyes tae focus. I was on my hands and knees. Air rasped into my chest with a wheeze. I wouldna win this fight, twas nae possible.

But I dinna want tae die — nae yet.

Nae without a chance tae—

I climbed tae my feet.

He hadna finished me which was goin' tae be a mistake. His biggest. He bragged, "I didn't want to kill you yet, Brother, our audience wants a good long fight."

I tried tae stay above my fury. My air was coming in bursts. I had tae calm myself. Unnnggghhhhhh, unnnggghhhhhh. I dinna take my eyes off his face, but kept my vision wide tae take in his movements.

He was good at distractin' me with false moves. I had tae anticipate the true one.

I watched his arm raise and swing. The arc was fast, but I

caught his hammer with my own. His weight shifted. His arm swung wide. It took a yell that forced all the air from my chest tae change my movement tae the other direction. I swung back and caught his abdomen, a glancin' blow but enough tae wind him. I stepped right, and though the pain was about tae drop me, swung a third time. I hit him in the shoulder and knocked him tae the ground.

The crowd chanted, "Magnus, Magnus, Magnus!"

He yelled, "Argh!" and dropped tae a knee but was up fast. He swung back at me, missing at first but forcin' me tae stumble back. The next swing hit my ribs on the other side and dropped me flat on my arse.

I dinna ken if I could get up. The top of the arena looked a great distance away and was all light and noise and nae — Kaitlyn's voice, thick and sexy, *can you see me?* — *Aye, I see you* — *What do you see?* — *my Kaitlyn* —

My brother swung down on me.

I blocked my face with my forearms, leaving my hammer tae the side, and tried tae roll out from under him.

His hammer hit my left arm and the pain was brutal but it knocked me back tae focus.

He had gone off balance.

In one movement I reached for my hammer, scrambled tae my feet and charged him. I was barely able tae breathe, and in so much pain — I lifted the hammer and brought it down square on his lower back, knockin' him stumblin' tae the ground.

I bellowed tae stay on top of my feet. I swung the hammer back and swung it down on him again, a crunch of bone, again and again and again, til he was on the ground, again and again, til he was barely movin' and again and again til he was nae movin' anymore.

I dropped my hammer and collapsed tae the ground beside

him flat on my back starin' at the sky. A clamor of noise around me and my vision was gone.

The chant, "Magnus, Magnus Magnus!" filled my head. The voice beside my ear said, "Your name is Magnus Archibald Caehlin Campbell. You are the heir to the throne of Donnan,"

I whispered the words, "My name is Magnus Archibald Caehlin—" Just before I blacked out from the pain.

A face swam intae focus above me.

I croaked out, "I live with Bella."

"Good," said the face and then I drowned under the pain again.

Kaitlyn holding her tartan under her throat, yellin' up at me, "My husband would know what to do. He would rescue me and hold me and apologize for all the asinine men of the world and he would never ever ever ever leave me."

Her eyes were focused on my chest, speaking tae my heart, nae lookin' up though I tried to lift her chin. "Please Kaitlyn, look up. Please."

"My husband would know what to do."

"Please, I beg of you."

"He would know."

"Please."

MAGNUS

*B*ella was waiting for me, sitting on the edge of my bed, when I limped intae my room.

"Welcome home, My Magnus." She looked intae my eyes and told me she missed me. Her hands ran down my shoulders and she pressed against my front.

"Ouch."

The guards, still standing at the door chuckled maliciously.

Without looking at them I said, "Donnan winna be king forever."

"He has many more sons." They left the room and the doors locked me in behind them.

Bella perched on one of our chairs. "First, you fought superbly, Magnus, really. I knew I was picking the right son. Very well done."

I grunted. I couldna move — standin', talkin', sittin', everything hurt.

"Would you like to lie down?"

"Aye, verra much, but—" I limped toward the bed.

She jumped up tae allow me tae lean on her arm and held me

steady while I dropped tae the bed with a groan. She knelt before me and lifted my feet tae the bed. The pain was intense in every part of my body. It took a moment of settling, allowing my body tae drop tae a lower position, before I could breathe again.

Bella climbed beside me on the bed and looked down on me. "So there are a few things I need to explain. We don't have much time."

"You look in a hurry, I winna be goin' anyplace soon. The doctor said I would be in bed for a couple of days."

"When I told you to get injured, I didn't mean quite so injured."

"You dinna tell me tae get injured — what are ye talkin' of?"

"Magnus I don't want to upset you, but you're a part of the resistance now."

"The resistance tae what?"

"To Donnan."

I tried tae read her face. "I daena think ye should be speakin' of—"

"When you were in the infirmary, you told the doctor that you lived with Bella, so he removed your patch. He replaced it with one being fed into our own network."

"The metal behind my ear?"

"Yes, if you hear a voice now, it's someone working for us. No one is listening to us anymore."

"Donnan will know, when I am nae respondin', they will know I altered it."

"Probably, but we have spics on the inside. We think we can hold them for about five days. It is unfortunate that you will be injured for two."

"I will be injured for longer than two. I am tae remain in bed for two. Then recoverin' for many days after — I winna be ready tae fight or... what are ye expectin' me tae do?"

"To kill Donnan, to kill him and take the crown."

I looked her in the eye. "If he discovers I have done this, that I am planning this, he will take it out on Kaitlyn. Twas nae right tae involve me without askin' me."

She glared down at me. "You are the next king and yet you lie here fretting over a 300-year-old girl? Magnus, a lot of scheming has gone into this. We have many lives at stake."

The pain was threatenin' tae pull me under. I took as deep a breath as I could. "I need another dose of the medicine and tae sleep. We can discuss this further in the morning."

KAITLYN

*Z*ach opened the door. "Katie! What are you — need something?"

"Nah, I was just — think I could come in? I was wondering if you could do something for me..."

"Sure, of course." He let me through the door. It had been a while since I had been here. A month since my anniversary. And then before that my visits were very rare.

That had been one of the good things about celebrating my anniversary with all of them, they left me alone more. Stopped being as worried about me. I guess in some ways I stopped being as worried too, but it was replaced with — what next?

A lot of nothing.

Ben's basket of toys was in the middle of the floor and some spilled over and across the rug. "Is Emma here?"

"She took Ben out for the afternoon. He has a Mommy and Me playgroup and then they were going to shop for dinner. Did you need her?"

"Nah." I sat at one of the bar stools at their kitchen island. It was a little depressing thinking about all the amazing food Zach made out of this little kitchen. He deserved the bigger one of our last house. He squinted his eyes at me then offered some cookies and milk.

I said, "As long as there's alcohol in my glass I'll take anything."

"Sure." He looked through the fridge and then through his liquor cabinet. "How 'bout Bailey's? I think that will go with chocolate chip cookies."

"Perfect." A moment later I had a plate of cookies and a glass in front of me.

Then he leaned on the kitchen counter and waited.

I chewed and then I drank.

Then I said, "I keep thinking about something you said the other day, that you Googled Magnus. I was wondering if you could tell me what you found?"

He nodded slowly. "Not much, Katie. I don't know if that's good news or not..."

"Can you show me? I can look myself but kind of think I need someone to do it with me, maybe to slam the laptop closed if I find something too... you know."

Zach's laptop was always open on the counter anyway so he swung it around and sat beside me on the next bar stool. He ran his hand through his hair. "What I found so far is not much — let's see, the Earl of Breadalbane."

"I met him."

"That is the weirdest crazy shit ever."

"It'll probably get weirder, maybe we should be high for this."

"No way, it might blow my mind so much I don't recover." He chuckled. "Okay, so here. Here's the Earl's family tree..."

"I don't know much, except Lizbeth, his niece."

"Could this be her, Elizabeth, wait, yes, her brother Sean, and this is her mother, Mairead."

"Whoa. So Magnus should..."

He turned the laptop to show me — Magnus. His birth year listed as 1681, then a dash — and blank. "It's blank."

I said, "It is. That's good news I think, right?"

"I have no idea. But here, Mairead is blank too."

"Okay, that means that... I have no idea. There should be a record."

"Though it says here that if there isn't a record it's simply because someone hasn't researched it yet."

I nodded. "Yeah, so it needs to be researched."

"That's why I was thinking we might want to go to Scotland. We could research it."

I gave him a sad smile. "I'd really like that. It's on my list to do when I become a bit better at this."

"You're doing really great."

"Thanks Zach, you have to say that, I'm your boss. What about Lizbeth, what does her...? I can't say it. Just tell me."

"She was married to Rory It looks like she had two children with him."

"What does it say about his death?"

"Just 1702."

"That's when I was there."

"Then she had a second husband, Liam. She married him in 1703."

I grinned, "Nice. She wanted him and she got him. Good for her."

"Except, I'm sorry Katie, she died later that year."

"Oh."

"And she had a son, four days before she died. In December 1703."

"Oh no."

Zach patted the back of my hand. "Have another cookie."

"What was her son's name?" I accidentally sprayed crumbs on his laptop. "Sorry. I'm not functioning very well."

"Her son's name was, Ainsley."

"Poor kid, to have your mom die when you're born. Did he at least have a long life, children?"

"Nope, he died when he was..." Zach counted on his fingers. "About two."

I sighed. "I didn't know Lizbeth long, but I really liked her."

"This is about all I can find here at my laptop. We could hire someone, a genealogist or something."

"Nice, 'genealogist' when did you get interested in this kind of stuff?"

"When we lost Magnus, I never thought about it before."

"When we lost Magnus..." I slammed the last of my Baileys. "You know, here's something, will you check the family tree for another older Magnus?"

"Really why?"

"They all called Magnus, 'Young Magnus,' and someone mentioned an older Magnus, but I never met him. And I don't know... is there anything?"

Zach spent a few minutes scrolling through the page searching small type for the name. Then he realized there was a handy search bar and he typed Magnus into it and the year and picked the location and, "All I can find is one."

"One Magnus?"

"I'll even do a date search and include all of Scotland, yeah, see, not a very popular name in Scotland in the seventeen hundreds."

"That is weird. I know I heard there was another Magnus that was old."

Zach's eyes went big. "Do you think it might have been our Magnus? That he was there, old, looped over himself, in the past of his past self? Oh shit, I'm not even high and you totally blew my mind."

"I'm not saying that at all. That totally sounds like something out of Star Trek. But I'm also saying, 'what if?' While trying really hard not to sound crazy."

Zach grinned. "I'm glad we don't sound crazy."

"We didn't really learn what happened to Magnus."

Zach closed the laptop lid. "We didn't learn much. But this was a big step for you. I'm impressed."

MAGNUS

 My doctor gave me permission tae leave the bed, but I was still in much discomfort and breathing was nae easy tae accomplish. I wanted tae go back tae bed, but Bella was receiving information from people close tae Donnan. We were expected at dinner tonight. And he was furious about something.

She said, "Probably the missing Tempus Omega, they are very precious."

"Couldna he make more?"

"No, they're an alien invention. He fought a war and won them. We don't know how to make anything that advanced."

"He keeps them all in one place?"

"Yes, in a room near his private apartments."

I scowled. I was in no mood for this errand, the conversation, this purpose. "You told me ye dinna ken the location of the vessels."

She smiled. It was silky and smooth and looked verra dishonest. "That was when I thought someone might be listening. You're on our side now. I can tell you anything because we work together." She ran her hand down my shoulder. "But it doesn't matter. It would be impossible to get a Tempus Omega with Donnan in charge, but if you kill him, if you're crowned king, you'll have access to all of them. All the wealth. Everything. Wouldn't that be perfect, My Magnus? Shouldn't that be your ultimate goal?"

"Och, aye. And there is a plan in place?"

"For Saturday night at the Gala during the dinner. You will kill him there. I need you to understand this is a very important night and many people are going to great lengths to help you. Like the doctor."

"Twas verra risky for him tae take off my patch."

"Yes, it was. So you understand that people are counting on you."

I inhaled deeply. "Aye."

Her hand rubbed down my arm. "At the dinner you will sit to Donnan's right. I will be beside you. If he tries to make me sit somewhere else, insist. I will have the gun and I'll pass it to you under the table. Do you know how to shoot?"

"My security guard trained me in shootin' in Florida, but how will ye have a gun? Dost ye have access tae weapons, can ye get me one now?"

She squinted her eyes. "If I had access to weapons, I would have killed Donnan years ago. Tanrick would have made a fine ruler, perhaps just as brutal but in different ways. There have been a number of sons who would have helped me. Trouble is they don't seem to survive. But you survived. Now we have hope and a plan and I'll have a weapon when the time comes."

I said, "You will have a gun from somewhere and ye will pass it tae me."

"This is the most important thing — you have to wait until the first course is eaten. Donnan's plate will be removed first. He likes to finish eating so he can make everyone else look as if they are too slow. It's his way to show his power. His plate will be taken. At that point there will be four guards behind you but one of them is with us. He will be ready. You will jump up and kill Donnan where he sits. Our guard will keep the other guards off you, but when you've done it you must return here to your rooms. Once Donnan is declared dead, you will emerge for your crowning."

"After I kill Donnan I will remain imprisoned?"

"For your protection." She went into the bathroom to put on her makeup, jars and sticks and brushes covered all the counter space and every shelf in my bathroom now. Not Kaitlyn's. Some strange woman named Bella that I couldn't even trust.

Guards led us along the passageways and down the elevator to the grand dining room. As we walked, I counted doors. I paused at a wall of windows lookin' over a forest at the back of the castle. The guards told me tae keep walking, but the sky was bright and I could make out the peaks on the horizon, one in particular had a distinctive shape.

Bella tugged at my arm. "What are you looking at, My Magnus?"

"Nothin', just the horizon. I haena seen it for many a day."

In the elevator, beside the buttons, the top floor was marked with a star. A guard pushed the button below it. I asked, "We arna goin' up tae Donnan's apartments?"

A guard grunted and said, "No, you don't get to go up there." The elevator doors opened on another hallway. I noted the door at the end, certain it was the stairwell, four doors down. It had been six doors tae the elevator. Donnan's apartments were on the top floor. I just had tae remember the way as soon as I dinna have four guards around me.

Finally we were pushed through to the dining room again. Donnan stood in the middle, a drink in hand. The table had three place settings at one end. He looked as if he was waiting for us.

"Magnus, my warrior, you've come to tell me of your latest battles!" He warmly shook my bound hands.

"I came because ye told me tae come."

"Exactly, like a good son. Have a seat." I took the chair tae his right. He held the chair for Bella at his left hand, then sat at the head.

I asked, "Will Lady Mairead be attendin' us?"

"No, she's traveling right now. She does love to plunder. For many years I used trained guards to collect for me, but it was not without hassles." He gestured for the server tae bring us wine. As they poured our glasses he said, "This wine is from 1242. It's not great, but when else have you ever imbibed a wine that was a thousand years old?"

He continued, "Where was I — your mother and her pilfering ways. The guards kept disappearing with my Tempus Omegas. I had to locate them again. It caused a great many difficulties. But Mairead is eminently trustworthy and capable." He rested his gaze on Bella's face, "I find myself missing her very much when she is gone."

Bella shook her hair. "But you miss me more, My Donnan?"

"Ah yes, I miss you more. But I've given you over to Magnus now. My warrior!" He turned his focus back tae me. "How are you healing, Son?"

"I will be ready tae fight when called upon."

"Good, good." Donnan stared at me long and then his starin' was interrupted by the arrival of our plates. "Speaking of needing to find my Tempus Omegas. Have you given any thought to where you may have hidden the one that was in your care?"

"Nae. I daena ken where it is."

"Daena ken? You don't know?" He turned tae Bella. "We

should really get his dialect sorted. There's no sense to be made of half of his words. Who was your speech coach, Bella, Reynolds?"

"Yes, but I think the way Magnus speaks is fine."

Donnan humphed. "Well, I suppose he is more of a warrior than an orator. The people seem to like him."

Eatin' with bound hands was difficult, but gave me something tae focus on instead of my rage.

Donnan's voice went slithery as it did just before he beat me with the stick last time. "It would mean a great deal to me if you would tell me where you put it... We could discuss the circumstances of your living situation. For instance I have a full stable with many glorious horses. You could ride."

"I canna tell ye where the vessel is. I daena ken the location, but I would verra much like tae ride."

Donnan wiped his hands on a napkin makin' me wait for a response. "The Tempus Omegas are very precious, Magnus. I have allowed you the use of one, but you haven't returned it. It's disrespectful."

"Twas lost. Nae sense in worryin' over it." I kept my eyes on the far wall, but kept my senses focused on his movement. He faced my side, the one most injured. All he would have tae do is hit me in the ribs and I would be in the infirmary again.

"Ah, but see, there is a reason to worry over it. In the hands of the wrong person much mischief could be done with these devices. It has been very difficult to keep them under my control." He tossed his napkin to the table beside his plate. "Since you aren't cooperating, I'll have to find it with the tracking signal."

"If it has a trackin' signal why dost ye keep askin' me for it?"

He smiled maliciously. "Finding it isn't precise. And once the signal is activated the Tempus Omegas could be located by anyone through time. I have to be ready to get to its location before someone else does."

He sat back in his chair with a sigh. "And there are wars raging in the South. Uprisings, resistance, political intrigues." He pushed his plate away from himself. "As the future king I thought you might want to save me the trouble and allow me to focus on the issues at hand. So I'll ask again, where is it?"

"I daena ken."

He nodded. "Bella, you'll attend me to my quarters tonight. I have a need for you."

"You canna have her, ye—"

Bella interrupted. "It's okay, My Magnus. I'll go with him tonight." She put her hand on Donnan's and looked up at him in a way that made my stomach turn.

Donnan said, "I'm done, don't hurry, Magnus, stay and enjoy the meal I've provided. I'll see you in three nights for my Autumnal Equinox Gala Dinner." He stood and said, "Come Bella."

She hastily dropped her fork mid-bite. "Of course." She took his arm. As they turned for the far door Bella said, "My Magnus, your beard is far more scruffy than I would like, see the barber tomorrow morning."

I scowled and watched as they left the room together.

I sat in quiet and finished eating my meal. Then I stood and the guards closed in around me and ushered me back to my quarters.

I did remember, though, tae recount the doors, checkin' the numbers tae make sure I had them in mind, and tae take note of the stairwell to Donnan's quarters again.

MAGNUS

The next morning Bella appeared at my door, comin' in with the breakfast plates. A plate of food for me and for her. She had a bruise on her cheek.

"Did he hit ye?"

"It's his way. He does that."

We ate in silence.

Finally she pushed the plate away. "Why didn't you argue more for me last night?"

"I tried tae. Ye said twas—"

"You looked weak. You sounded like you didn't care for me at all. Donnan made jokes about it. About how I was worthless. How you didn't want me."

"I..." I dinna ken how tae answer the charge. There was nae answer that would help.

She watched my face then hastily said, "You should get me pregnant. If I was the mother of the heir to Donnan's throne, he wouldn't just take me like that. I would get more respect."

"I am married."

She stood and shoved plates off the table clattering all over the floor. "She is dead. Dead, Magnus. And you are mine, so stop being such a fool and be a king already." She paused at the bathroom door. "Don't make me regret choosing you."

I don't know how she arranged it, but when our breakfast plates were cleared four guards stood outside my room tae accompany me tae the barber.

He cut my hair. He trimmed my beard. He filled the surrounding air with sweet scents and aromatic oils. He massaged my scalp and shoulders until I winced as he moved down my back. "Tis too painful."

"Certainly, Magnus." He worked on my shoulders again. "I watched the fight, very good. You'll make a fine king someday."

I asked, "That is all it takes, killin' in an arena?"

He chuckled as he wiped along my neckline and jaw with a soft towel. "Are you living alone?"

I said, my eyes closed and without much thinkin' on it, "Nae, I live with Bella now." I felt something heavy drop tae my lap. I glanced down. Twas a gun inside a leather holster. While he stood wiping my jaw, fussin' with the hair at the sides of my ears, I fumbled it intae my kilt, under my belt, hidden and secure. It reminded me of that time Kaitlyn was applyin' the bandage tae my forehead while I pulled the knife from under her skirt — *I love you strong as an oak, near a stone wall, aligned with a castle tower* — just before she...

The guards returned me tae my room.

KAITLYN

*H*ayley yelled, "Katie!" when I walked out to the back deck of James's house.

"Hi, everyone," I said with as much enthusiasm as I could. Then I endured the hugs. But that was a lie — the hugs were nice.

Hayley said, "You came to the 'End of October Not Halloween Party!' We didn't even have to come get you. I'm so freaking proud of you."

I joked, "Quentin drove, it wasn't all bravery."

Quentin walked in a step behind. "I handcuffed her and forced her into the car." I batted him on the arm.

Zach and Emma entered a moment later and soon there was a full blown party. Barbecue, beer, shots. James had broken up with his girlfriend and no one could remember which of them slept around first, or the most, but it had been dramatic and seemed permanent. It was very nice not having her around so he could be fun to talk to again. Our friendship had been nonexistent for months and months but he was trying to be a part of our gang again.

Our gang. I was trying to be a part of it again too.

It was hard, but it was also time. And yesterday was the one-year anniversary of Magnus leaving. It hadn't been an easy day, but also, it hadn't been the worst. It was just a day, time ticking by. He wasn't here and the truth was, he wasn't going to be here. Probably. Not anymore.

With each day I could get a little more used to thinking it.

There had been many a day that I wanted to move to Los Angeles or some other place that didn't remind me constantly of Magnus, but I couldn't leave my grandma. Or Zach and Emma and Quentin and Baby Ben. Hayley. They were all my family now. I had to take care of them. It was ironic because they had been taking care of me for so long.

I assumed a position on James's deck, perched on the railing. I had been coming here since I was a kid. A long long time. The dunes had barely changed in all those years. Shifting a bit, but not noticeably from this direction.

Yet the beach side was eroded. Fall storms had washed away a good portion of the dunes.

It was weird how from one viewpoint the beach was unchanged, but if I walked out on the sand and looked back at the house the dunes looked drastically different. Different viewpoints, different experiences, in the same place, different times.

My time period was this, surrounded by friends, helped by my chosen family, full of food and drinks and kindness and support, and what was Magnus doing? What was his time full of? It should be time spent here with me. What else were our vows for?

And he made me a vow.

He promised to love me until death do us part.

This was where I kept coming to these days — he promised me.

And still he left.

Michael walked in with Tyler. I caught Hayley's eye and mouthed, "Why the hell is he here?"

She rolled her eyes and hugged them hello. Now that Michael and Tyler had become close friends I was thrown together with him every couple of weeks. Hayley came to stand beside me.

I asked again, "Why is he here?"

"Because it's a party, because he's friends with Michael, because you're nice enough to let his personality slide..."

"He mansplains to me all the time. I've never met anyone so infuriating in my life. It's like he thinks I'm an idiot."

She giggled and turned so he couldn't tell we were talking about him. "He just thinks you're a sad lost case he needs to help. Like a puppy. And he mansplains to me too, it's just his way. Last week he told me how to use Google Docs. I've been using Google Docs for two years, in my business, my flourishing—"

"Shhhh, he's coming over."

Tyler said, "Hey Katie."

"Hi Tyler, back visiting the Island again?"

"Yep, there's a lot about this island that draws me back."

"Me too. Careful, you'll become a local and all you'll talk about is real estate and football."

"I'm from New York that's all we talk about there too. And I don't know, it doesn't sound that bad." He leaned against the railing. "How have you been this week? I heard it was a tough anniversary for you."

"Yeah, it's been a rough one. I burrowed under a pile of work to get through it. I changed my investment strategy and directed my portfolio toward—"

"I remember you talking about that idea a couple of weeks ago. I was thinking about it, you should really hire a money manager. An investment advisor could help you get a new strategy. You don't want to lose money."

"Yeah of course not — hey that's a great idea, I should do that." I took a swig from my beer using the bottle to hide my rolling eyes.

Hayley saw it. "Be nice."

I whispered, "Be nice? Be nice? Why the hell should I be nice?"

He seemed oblivious to my irritation. "I was also thinking about your situation with all these employees, it might be useful for you to—"

"Wait, did you hear that — James? Did you call me? Hold on, James is calling me." I slid down from the railing and crossed to the other side of the deck. I stood beside the grill making James block Tyler's view of me.

I whispered, "Save me."

James said, "From who, Tyler?"

"Yes, how'd you guess?"

"Tyler's great. What's wrong with Tyler?"

"He mansplains everything to me. It's irritating."

"God, you're such a feminist. You know what you should do is—"

"You're mansplaining! I know what I should do, I should hide behind you until he goes home." I giggled.

James laughed. "Yeah, what the hell do I know? I can *not* figure out women."

"Oh god, stop with that already. You can too figure out women. Women want a guy who loves them and doesn't sleep around with other women. Period. Did you love Lee Ann?"

"Yes."

"Did you sleep around with other women?"

"Just that one time but—"

"Then you don't get her. You don't get Lee Ann. She's done. Now next time you meet someone and you really like her, maybe even love her, are you going to sleep with other women?"

"I don't know..."

"See, until you can say, 'No. I won't sleep with other women,' you don't get to say, 'I love her.' That's your bad. And you're smart enough to know this."

"I know, I don't know why I do it." He flipped the burgers on the grill.

"I know why you do it, because you get scared of the idea of loving just one person. It terrifies you so you sabotage yourself. You have an affair so when your relationship ends you won't be hurt."

He chuckled.

"What?"

"You're woman-splaining. Maybe I just like women, lots of women. Maybe I hate the idea of one woman forever."

I slowly shook my head. "Have I told you today how grateful I am that we broke up?"

James announced, "Burgers are ready!" and piled the burgers on a plate.

It cooled off considerably as the sun went down so we left the deck for the indoors. We sat around the dining room table and talked and laughed. It felt really good to be surrounded by friends. And Hayley was right, I needed to get out more often. Even if it meant spending time with Tyler.

I kept catching him looking at me. I would need to deal with that later. Send some clear messages of the 'not interested' variety.

Hayley said, "So Michael, you and Tyler are going out in the boat tomorrow?"

"Yeah, we were going to go fishing. I should check the weather though, there's a front moving in."

He pulled his phone from his pocket but Tyler interrupted. "I've got weather alerts set up, I'll check." He clicked and scrolled. "Let's see, um..." Then he said, "Have you guys been watching this story about the insane storms in Scotland?"

I choked on a big swig of beer.

I coughed for a full minute before I said, "What did you say? What?"

Tyler said, "These insane storms in Scotland. They're huge, building over this one village and then they stop. They start at the same time every day. It's been like a week. You haven't been following the news?"

I stood. "Like an electrical storm? What's the name of the village?"

While everyone else looked from my face to his, Tyler said, "Totally electrical." He read for a moment, then said, "The village is... let's see... you're not going to believe this name, near Spittal of Glenshee. There's a ruin there, a Talsworth Castle."

"Quentin can you take us home?" I grabbed my jacket off the back of my chair and pushed my arms into the sleeves.

Hayley said, "What is it — Magnus?"

"That's the village where he's from, it..."

Emma rushed down the hall to scoop Baby Ben from the guest room bed and carried him sleeping to the front door where Quentin was already waiting.

Tyler asked, "Wait, Katie, you have to leave?"

"Yeah um, that's the village, it's..."

Quentin opened the door and headed out to the car followed by Zach and Emma.

James shrugged. "Maybe that's why Magnus was so freaked out by storms. The storms in Scotland get so freaky they get international coverage."

Hayley said, "Call me tonight, let me know what's going on."

As I left, Tyler said to James. "But I thought he left her. Why is she worried about the storms over his village?"

I raced down the stairs to the car.

"That's the village, Quentin, the village where the ruins of Talsworth are located. Why would storms be happening in 2018 there unless it's Magnus? What if he's trying to come through, and he's just coming there instead of here and maybe something — why are you driving so slow?"

"I'm following the speed limit so I can get you home alive so we can figure this out."

A text message happened, Hayley: Tell me everything.

Mine: That's the village, right beside the castle ruins. Where Lady Mairead lived. Those storms.

I wasn't making sense.

I was scrolling over Scotland's weather, but the problem with weather.com was every time you looked at it new stories were at the top of the page. I finally found it.

"Look at the photo Quentin." I held my phone up so Quentin could look while he was driving. I showed it to Emma and Zach in the back seat. "Just look, it looks exactly like the storms."

I typed Scotland storms into news and came up with photo after photo of tall banking clouds and electrical arcs of lightning. I read out loud, "'Every day at the same time.' It's like he's trying to tell me something. To send me a message. I have to go."

Quentin nodded. "We have to go."

I texted Hayley: It's got to be Magnus. I have to go to Scotland.

BEGIN WHERE WE ARE | 111

She texted back: When?

Maybe tomorrow.

Don't go without talking to me first, I'll come with you.

Really?

Really. Just text me the details.

KAITLYN

$\mathcal{B}$ack at my apartment, Zach and Quentin and I came up with a plan. Zach would stay in Florida. He and Emma would be here in case Magnus showed up. Also to handle any business/house/life things that needed to be handled. And finally, in case I found Magnus but needed lawyers, banks, or specialists of some kind, it would be good to have someone on the ground at home who could handle the research or phone calls or whatever it would take. Extradition? Importing? How would we get him home without a passport? I didn't want to worry about it yet.

Plus, none of us wanted to take Zach without Emma or Emma without Ben and I had no idea what we were about to find. It didn't seem wise to take Ben into an unknown.

I called Hayley and confirmed that she would get on a plane with me the next day. She said yes. I told her she was saying that because she had been drinking and she would be pissed when I woke her up to go to the airport in six hours.

She told me that she would be ready to go, with a lot of complaints about my lack of trust.

I bought three tickets to Edinburgh, departing in seven hours. Quentin went to his apartment to pack.

I packed my bags fueled by excitement. All I knew was that Magnus was coming home. That's what this meant. The storms — he was coming home.

MAGNUS

I had nothin' tae do. I couldna train, I could barely breathe from the ache in my ribs. All I did was rest. I went tae the gym and walked the track for a while concentratin' on my breathin' and my worries.

I wasna physically ready tae overthrow the king. I had gotten my arse kicked as Master Quentin would say. I won, but barely. I wasna ready.

Bella had a plan in motion though and it was happenin'. I needed tae make m'self ready.

When I returned tae my room, Bella was lounged on my bed, facin' the door, waitin' for me.

I sat on the edge of the bed. "My apologies I dinna argue for ye last night, Bella. I dinna ken the rules of Donnan's game."

She sat up against the headboard. "There's only one rule with Donnan, he is the one with all the power. But you're the next king, you should challenge him. Especially over me."

I nodded and looked down at the wedding band on my left hand. "I haena lied tae ye about bein' married. I am nae lookin' for a new wife. You say Kaitlyn is dead, but I canna think of her as gone. She is alive in my heart and tis enough for me."

She looked petulant and flicked the covers tae the side. "We've been sharing a bed, living together, and you're telling me you don't want me? You are so weak."

"I am tellin' ye that I am married. Tis nae weakness.

She huffed and rose from the bed in a fury. "So what, I have to return to Donnan?"

"Nae, I will protect ye. I winna let him have ye anymore. I think that is enough."

"It's not enough." She banged on the door. "Guards, let me out!"

I grabbed her elbow. "Bella, what are ye doin'?"

"I'm leaving. I'll go back to Donnan. I'd rather do that than be here with you."

"You canna go back tae Donnan. We have a plan, twill nae work if ye go back tae him."

She raised her chin as imperiously as she could. "Tell me, am I yours? In the future, when you are the king, will I be your wife, your queen?"

"I have told ye, tis nae possible, I am married tae Kaitlyn."

"Stop saying her name! Stop saying her name to me! You make me sick." She banged through the bathroom doorway again and slammed the door leavin' me alone in the room.

KAITLYN

First of all, as predicted, Hayley was not happy when we arrived at her door at 4:35 am.

Her suitcase was packed, but she was completely crashed. Quentin stood at the front door checking his watch, while I cajoled her out of bed, into sweatpants and a T-shirt, and put on her shoes. "You're acting like Ben, you're making me put your shoes on like Ben. And he's a one-year-old."

She twisted her hair up in a messy bun, yawned, and said, "I'm only saying this because I'm his aunt, but he is very manipulative."

"Says the grown ass woman who has another grown ass woman tying her shoes, for no other good reason than she's too tired."

"I also drank too much. I need to address that."

"This is a recurring theme with you. Stop addressing how much you need to address it and do something about it." I tied the last bow. And blew toward my forehead. Hot work struggling shoes on a grown ass woman who wasn't in a helpful mood. "Thank you for coming with me by the way. It means a lot."

"I know and it better, you owe me big." She collapsed back on the bed, moaned, struggled over to the side, pulled herself up way-dramatically, and finally lumbered to her feet with a groan. "What time is it?"

"4:43, we have to hit the road."

"How did you talk me into this?"

"Magnus," I said as I jogged down the steps to the car.

An hour and twenty minutes later we were boarding our flight. I had a full blown sweat going by the time I dropped into the middle seat. Quentin took the aisle like a good security guard. Hayley got the window seat, yanked the shade down, put her head on my shoulder, and fell asleep immediately. I rested my cheek on her head and tried to do the same.

Quentin hooked his thumbs on his thighs and planted himself, still and watchful. He didn't move and barely blinked. I teased him about it usually, that he was like the British guards in front of the royal palace, unmovable and unflappably calm. He told me that was why Magnus hired him, which wasn't wrong.

He did finally fall asleep with his head lolling. I jiggled him awake to give him the neck pillow I bought for myself. Who was I kidding bringing it? After an hour of exhausted passing out, I was too excited to sleep.

We had a layover in New York. Then we flew directly to Edinburgh. We rented a car and it was in the car that Hayley finally woke up.

"So where are we, actually?"

"You've just gone through three airports and a car rental—"

Quentin joked, "A car hire."

I chuckled, "A car hire, and now Quentin—"

He interrupted again, "Stop talking to me. I'm driving on the wrong side of the road. It's taking all my concentration."

Hayley joked, "I was wondering what was going on, figured I was sitting in the car upside down again." She yawned and straightened up in her seat. "Where are we headed?"

"Eastern Perth and Kinross, near the Spittal of Glenshee. If that helps at all." I was looking at the map the car hire people gave us, because come to find out our phones didn't have much cell service and it was a lot like being in Scotland in the eighteenth century. I loud-whispered to Hayley in the backseat, "Shhhhh, Quentin is driving. We'll be there in about an hour. Of course he's driving at half the speed limit so maybe longer."

"Look at the speed limit signs. I'm doing all this math in my head."

"You don't have to do any math. You just have to look at the dial and correspond it to the sign, brainiac."

He chuckled. "Oh yeah, right. Man, I'm tired. I'm not thinking right."

Hayley said, "How did I get through the airport?"

"You woke up enough to smile at the passport guy and hand him your passport. He only thought I was people-trafficking you a little bit."

"When do we get to our hotel?"

"I haven't booked one yet, this is a very classy operation."

"So basically our security guard with questionable driving skills is taking us to the middle of Scotland to the ruins of a castle to look for a time machine? And we might be homeless?"

"You're catching on. It should be easy to find the ruins too, they are strung with caution tape. We may have to sneak in."

"Can I go back to sleep?" She wadded up one of the jackets.

"That's why you're in the back seat."

~

We took two wrong turns and had to stop for directions but we finally found the correct Unnamed Road with the Historic Sites sign and followed it to the ruins of Talsworth Castle. The parking lot was empty. The ticket booth was empty. A sign on the front said, 'closed.' Caution tape stretched across the foot path. Absolutely nothing looked familiar to me from 1702. Nothing. Just a path going past the ticket booth and a sign that showed a couple of walking trails.

"What time is the storm usually?" asked Quentin.

"The news story said it happens at 4:15 pm every day. So about three hours from now."

Quentin looked around. "Should we risk leaving the car here? Someone might come by and investigate. We don't want to be found before we see the storm, or whatever it is we're looking for."

"Now that I'm here I actually have no idea what I'm looking for or why. This sounds really crazy."

Hayley said, "If you think about it you're like a storm chaser."

"Well, that sounds better than 'insane person'."

Quentin said, "How about I park back where the road branches away and we hike in?" I took a photo of the trail map and we returned to the car.

~

We had been hiking for a while before Hayley started complaining. "Where the hell is a pub? Isn't that why people come to Scotland? I'm in Scotland and so far all I've seen is trees and hills. A couple of farms. Now I'm on a hike. If I wanted to hike, I'd go on the Appalachian trail."

Quentin bantered with her. "Would you? I mean seriously, I don't think you're much for camping or the outdoors."

"Yeah, you're right, I hate being in nature. I just had such a good complaint going I forgot to make sense." She laughed. We all laughed.

A few moments later the small woods opened up and we had a view of the front partial wall of the castle. "Oh!"

My memory filled in the missing spots — Talsworth.

It hit me all at once: the long ago past, the castle, riding towards it with Magnus behind me on the horse, all the fear.

"Oh," I said again, staring up at what was left of the walls. "I don't know what to..."

Quentin asked, "Does it look familiar?"

"Yeah, this is the castle. I stood right here three hundred plus years ago."

"Let's walk around the grounds, maybe we'll get a feeling for the best place to watch the storm."

"How long have we got left?"

"Two hours."

We walked up to the front gate now nothing more than a partial wall with a section of a tower in one corner. We walked across the courtyard to the staircase where I met Lord Delapointe that first time. *Kaitlyn Campbell! Well, well, a daughter!* Him and his sleazy smile. Now the staircase climbed toward nothing.

There was an enclosed hall near the back of the square but that was really it. I took in the scope of it turning around. I said, "It was so big before, it towered over the land. We were up on the second floor, trapped in Lord Delapointe's office, and I didn't think I would be able to escape." — *I love you, strong as an oak, near a stone wall, aligned with a castle tower* — I stopped dead in my tracks.

Hayley asked, "What did you...?"

"Maybe it's not — maybe it's..."

Quentin asked, "Maybe it's what?"

"The thingy, maybe it's..." I ran toward the right tower and scanned the clearing ahead of it. The distance was about right, though nothing looked familiar, manicured grass and pebbled paths. I ran towards the woods.

Quentin followed.

Hayley called, "Why are we running now? Aren't we going to sit here and wait for the storm?"

"Stop asking dumb questions and follow me!"

The woods were manicured. The underbrush was cleared. The first rows of trees were more like garden trees than woods.

I turned left, walked for a bit, and looked back at the castle. The tower that I needed to judge by was not there anymore, just the base of it, but I aimed my sights on the blank space above it. My guess was I was still too close. I backed up, my heart racing. I brisk-walked backwards even farther.

The tower was still visible, but that wasn't necessarily good — I scanned the area for the oak tree. There was one to my right, much larger than before. I looked up at the branches. There was nothing familiar about it. I turned away to locate the stone wall.

I found it, almost hidden behind bushes, a stone wall crumbling in places.

By now Quentin wanted to know what was happening.

"It's the wall." I scrambled over it.

"I see, you're going over a wall."

Hayley said, "What's up with the wall is what we're asking?"

"It's where Magnus hid the time vessel for me last time. What if it's here? What if I'm about to find it? What if it's been messaging me to come to him? What if?"

The inside corner was built up higher than the outside, dirt and leaves and lichen and — I popped my head up. "Got anything to dig with?" Quentin climbed over to join me in the corner.

"TSA stole my shovel," he joked looking for a rock with a sharp end. "Use this."

Hayley climbed over the wall and watched while sipping from her water. I scraped at the earth. The top layer was soft above hard layers that didn't want to move. I passed the stone to Quentin and he scraped and dug for a few moments.

I said, "My turn again," and kept digging until I had gone pretty deep. Like inches deep. And then I dug more.

Hayley asked, "You think something will really be there?" I mean, couldn't we watch, see if the storm is centered here? Maybe it's somewhere else?"

I stood and rested and blew the hair from my face. I was sweating and really tired. And now mucked up and totally dirty.

Quentin asked, "Want me to dig, Katie?"

"I should do it so if nothing's here I won't feel guilty."

I went back to digging on my knees in the dirt, scraping with the stone, using all my strength and then — clunk. My stone hit metal. "Oh my god, oh my god, oh my god." I had my hand on Magnus's time travel vessel. "It's here, oh my god." I gingerly pulled it up from the muck and mire of three hundred years.

Hayley asked, "What does this mean?"

"I don't know." I leaned on the wall with the vessel cradled in my hands. "I don't know. What does this mean? Magnus left it here for me. Or, he left it here. Definitely. Probably for me."

"What are you going to do with it now that you've found it?"

"I have no idea."

I stared down at it.

Quentin said, "Would you go to the past? To 1702? I mean, probably — right?"

I looked at him working it through my mind. "Yeah, 1702, I mean that's all I've got. The only numbers I know. Let me make sure it works." I twisted the ends and the vessel purred to life. The markings glowed around the middle.

Quentin said, "I should go with you — Magnus wouldn't want you to go alone. I'm not supposed to leave your side and..."

"No, I don't think that's a good idea."

"I don't want to explain to Magnus after I let you go through time by yourself. So I might as well quit now."

I huffed. "Okay, fine. But as soon as I find him we'll send you right back."

"What about me?" asked Hayley. "I'm just supposed to get myself home from Scotland? Freaking Scotland? We're in some kind of primordial forest and the only way home is driving a car on the wrong side of the street?"

I said, "Here's what you're going to do. You'll drive the car to Edinburgh. Call Emma. She'll buy you a ticket home. Stay in a really nice hotel. Go to a pub. Be the cool girl out on the town in a foreign country. Turn the car back in. Get our stuff. Fly home with it."

Quentin climbed over the wall and jogged across to our packs and rifled through them moving the car keys and the paperwork into Hayley's bag.

Hayley nodded, "Okay, I can do that but you seriously owe me. You owe me a trip to Europe with you. When Magnus is home we'll leave him in charge of the house and you'll go on a trip with me because you owe me big."

I smiled, "Definitely, I owe you — "

A loud thunderous boom filled the air, and lightning struck the oak tree right beside Quentin. The tree caught fire and flames spread from branch to branch. Quentin said, "Holy shit!" and rushed toward me but he was too late.

The wind whipped around me and like a cannonball a force hit me in the stomach, pulled the air from my lungs, tore me to pieces, and then it got really really really bad.

MAGNUS

Bella was petulant for the rest of the day. She sulked around the room and stayed verra long in the bathroom. Twas nae easy tae live with her.

At dinner we ate in silence until I began tae speak of the plan. I knew the guards had guns and I was nae happy with the prospect of being shot. "You are sure the guard will be able tae keep me from harm?"

She scowled. "If you do your part, shoot Donnan, the guards won't hurt you. You'll be the next king. Why would they risk your revenge? So what are you going to do?"

"Shoot him."

"Exactly." She watched me for a moment then languidly sighed. "This would be much better if we were planning our ascension together. Can't we?"

I shook my head.

She stood and walked around the table trailin' a finger along the table top and then up my neck tae my chin. She clasped my chin in her hands and forced me tae look up in her face. "Think about this, My Magnus." She leaned down and kissed me, pressing against my mouth and bitin' my lips. I tried tae turn my head but she pulled and bit and then she whispered, her breath enterin' my wounded lungs, "I could take care of you. I would like that." She straddled my lap and sat down.

I groaned.

"And we would be together, me and you." She forced my chin up and kissed along the edge of my neck.

"We have spoken of this, you and I, ye ken the reason—"

She pressed her lips tae my mouth stoppin' my words. "We haven't truly spoken of this yet, My Magnus." She pulled my chin so she was looking intae my eyes. "We haven't spoken of the plan you have to kill Donnan, how you are planning to take his throne. We haven't spoken of it yet, about how I know this is what you are planning. That I know all about your plan and Donnan still doesn't know."

"What are ye sayin'?" Rage filled my chest.

"I am saying that I know your plans. I know everything about you. I know that you have a gun. We have secrets that we keep together. And being together is—"

"Are ye sayin' you will tell Donnan about your plans, Bella?" She raised up a bit, kissing me, tugging my shirt up over my head. I grimaced from the pain of it. My ribs were hurtin' terribly. "Is that what you're sayin'?"

She ran her hands down my chest and kissed along my collarbone. "I wouldn't want to Magnus, I would never want to do anything to hurt you. You're My Magnus, my warrior." She raised her hips and pulled my kilt up tae my waist. "And you want me." Her hand wrapped around my cock and pulled it firm tae her front.

"I promised I would protect ye, you daena have tae resort tae threats."

"Yes, My Magnus, but I want more than protection. I want you." Her breath was comin' heavy in my ear. "You want me.

They aren't threats, they are simply reminders that you have a secret. And that I will keep it if I'm happy, but I could go to Donnan if I wanted to."

"Ye would go tae Donnan and tell him?"

"Only if you refuse me."

She kissed along my throat and her hips raised and lowered causing a much missed friction. My breaths were comin' fast. She whispered against my skin, "You want me. You want to survive. You will be king. And Kaitlyn has been dead for centuries."

I closed my eyes. "Stop speakin' of Kaitlyn."

"True," she put her weight on one leg, dragged her panties down with one hand, stepped out of them, and stepped across my lap again. She sat back down with a soft breath against my ear. "I said that to you just yesterday. And we shouldn't talk of her because she doesn't matter. Not to you. Because you and I have secrets. We keep them."

"If you tell Donnan her life would be in danger, you know that, how could you?"

She pulled her shirt, little more than a strip of cloth, off over her head. "I don't want her to be in danger. I'll help you keep her safe. It will be easier if I'm happy. That's all I'm saying." She raised and lowered again. "I learned about her, you know. I saw photos. She had a child, a long happy life without you, she died old and—"

"Stop speaking of her!" Enraged, grabbing her around the arse, I stood, my fingers digging intae the flesh of her. I lifted her tae the bed and threw her on the mattress.

She squealed happily, makin' me even more furious. "I told you you wanted me."

"I daena want ye."

"Oh yes you do, you want me because you want to live, you want to be king, and you want to survive."

"Stop sayin' it."

"I won't, without me you're a dead man. Without me, Kaitlyn doesn't live to meet her child. She bedded someone else, why are you—"

I pushed my kilt tae the ground, lunged onto her, shoved her legs apart and pushed intae her and used her against all my fury. She held on and wrapped her legs around my back and bit intae my shoulder.

When I finished, I shoved away and sat at the edge of the bed. She rubbed a foot along my thigh. I pushed it aside. "Daena touch me."

I tried tae catch my breath, twas too fast from exertion and anger. I doubled over and tried tae calm m'self down.

She stretched long on my bed watching me try tae overcome the pain of breaths comin' and goin' within a chest that had been much abused.

"Are you okay, My Magnus?"

I swallowed a deep breath and held it long then exhaled slowly. I pulled my kilt off the floor, stepped intae the center of it, and managed tae get it on with a lot of effort.

There was nae puttin' on the shirt my middle was in too much pain. "You winna ever threaten me again."

"I won't, My Magnus."

"And ye winna go tae Donnan anymore. Not anymore. I winna stand for it."

The edge of her lips curled up a bit. "I won't need to, I'm truly yours now."

KAITLYN

When I pulled my conscious self up from the place of pain where I had been writhing and screaming forever it seemed, I felt trapped. The pain was red hot and I was sweaty, stifled, and weighed down.

My eyes were clamped shut, but it wasn't dark in my head. It felt burning bright around me, like if I opened my eyes they would burn to ash. There was flesh on my skin. I was skin to skin, a movement — my breath caught, what the fuck was — I forced my eyes open, skin, freckled, spotted, a shoulder against my chin, butting against my chin and he—? Oh my god, a man was on me, fingers on my neck, a hot stinking breath against my temple, holy fuck he was inside me. I struggled and wiggled against the body. The light so bright I couldn't see past the few inches of strange skin in front of my face. "Let me go, let me — get off me." My voice was small and pleading against the incredibly loud strange-man's breath ringing in my ears and his grunts as he pushed against me.

It was really hard to get my arms to move. In pain and weak, I flailed trying to beat his back. I bucked against him trying to get him off my body. "Get off me, get off me!" but he wasn't stopping. I begged and cried until the man finished using me. He pulled away with a satisfied pat on my hip.

My eyes still closed, I scrambled to the headboard of the bed, wrapped my arms around my face and cried again for longer.

Tears streamed from my eyes, the trauma, the bright lights, but I squinted trying to understand where I was, what I was dealing with. The light all around me was white and so bright it made the details indiscernible. In the hazy middle at the end of the bed a man was dressing,

I said, "Give me my fucking clothes."

He was big, broad shouldered, his hair light. I guessed he was in his late forties. Except for his lightness there was a familiarity to Magnus that made my stomach drop.

His smile, spread across his face, was ice cold. "Your clothes are filthy. And now that you're a guest here you won't need them. I prefer you naked." He chuckled.

Pain tears swam down my cheeks. I clamped my eyes shut and tucked into my knee caps. "Who are you?" My voice echoed in my ears. I pressed my hands over them, sniveling into the space between my knees.

"I'm Donnan. Your king. Stay on the bed you'll be needed later." He made to leave.

Squinting I made out the door, his hand on the door handle. "Why am I here, why are you keeping me?"

"You stole something of mine. The penalty is death, but you seemed too obliging to kill."

MAGNUS

Kaitlyn was at the end of Barb and Jack's dock. "One, two, three!" She held her nose and jumped with a squeal of laughter. As the water splashed and covered her over, my heart sank. "Kaitlyn!" I thundered down the boards tae the end. She was under the water, swimmin' up, but nae swimmin' up, strugglin', as if something held her fast under the water.

I dropped tae my knees and reached down splashin', trying tae grasp her flailing arms. "Grab my arm! Grab it, I'll pull you up!" She continued strugglin' just below my reach. "Grab it Kaitlyn, grab my arm." She slowly stopped struggling and sank away—

"Kaitlyn!"

I woke with a start sitting up in bed. The act of it distressed my injured ribs knockin' my air out again. "Och nae."

Bella's voice in the darkness, "My Magnus, are you okay?"

It took a moment for my voice to travel from inside the pain of my body to outside in the air. "Nae."

She dramatically sighed.

"I am nae good enough tae overthrow the crown. I need more time."

"You can't have more time. It's now. You'll have to find the strength. Donnan looks weak compared to you. People like you. You've won battles and it's time. The Autumnal Equinox Gala is the place to do it."

I scowled.

She rose up on her knees and rubbed my forehead, pushing away the wrinkles there. "I know you're worried. But everything is in place. You just have to kill him and get back here. We'll take care of the rest of it."

"And by we, you mean?"

"The resistance. All of us, we will—"

"And when I return here, how long before I am free tae take the throne?"

"I don't know how long, Magnus. I would think a few days? It depends on who is here to contest your ascension."

A pile of clothes was delivered tae me while I was in the infirmary. I had been feelin' verra hot and the pain on breathin' was terrible. I spent a time with an air mask feedin' my lungs until I felt a little better. The doctor told me nae tae go tae the Gala, but I had tae go. Twas my duty as the prince.

The other stuff I was plannin' that was the extra I wasna sure I could do.

I stared down at the clothes. They were in the fabric of the time, soft and flimsy, stretching, and form fitting but in the style of my own. A kilt, just in something resemblin' silk. Bella walked intae the room as I was investigatin' it.

"Tis nae enough fabric tae cover m'pikestaff."

"That's why you wear the undergarments, for layers." She admired me and ran a hand down my back.

"Undergarments with a kilt? Twould be an embarrassment. What would I do at the Gala when I want tae relieve myself?"

"You plan to relieve yourself at Donnan the Second's Autumnal Equinox Gala Dinner? Do we need to go over your manners again?"

"Och, nae more lessons. I will behave like a — "

Are you a barbarian Magnus, is that what you are?

"—I'll behave."

"Good. Just until your murderous rampage and then you can do whatever you want. And after, you can have me all you want."

I stepped intae the kilt and pulled it up. And then, because the fabric was so flimsy, I pulled on the undergarments. Twas a tiny pair of wee tight shorts. I was reminded of that night, long ago, plannin' with Kaitlyn to travel to the past together. Gatherin' with our friends tae organize our supplies and laughing about the shorts, teasin' Michael about his new hobby.

How long had it been?

Time had gone so much faster in Kaitlyn's present. The days slipped by as I was experiencing hours in my own time, but this was nae my time nor Kaitlyn's. I had a vague sense of dread that many many years had passed. That the truth of Kaitlyn's life, the baby with another man, the aging of her, had happened already.

And it had.

She had lived it through.

Once I killed Donnan, Bella wanted tae have me locked up here, tae wait until I was called upon. But I wouldna wait anymore. Killing Donnan would give me the right tae own the vessels. I would take all of them and disappear intae the past. I would go tae Kaitlyn. I would try verra hard tae get there before she decided tae live without me. I buckled on my sporran. It was as empty as my life now.

KAITLYN

*L*ady Mairead's voice came to me through the covers that were pulled tight around my head. Only my face peeking out, facing the door, trying to keep my eyes closed but also wanting to be alerted when that man showed back up.

"Explain tae me how ye came tae be in Donnan's bed?"

Her eyes were furious.

"Please, help me." I scrambled up to sitting and clasped my hands. "Please. I don't know who he is. I don't know why I'm here. I found one of the vessels and woke up here. He's holding me captive, and this—" I gestured toward a slice on my left cheek. "I woke up and this was here." The cut scared the hell out of me when I used the bathroom. My cut matched Lady Mairead's scars. "He's a monster. You have to help me."

"He," Lady Mairead said imperiously, "is Magnus's father. And ye will kindly quit your speakin' on the matter. Your presence complicates things verra much."

She exhaled angrily. "But perhaps now Magnus will see how ye are always conniving tae get what ye want."

"Magnus is here?" My hands still clasped I begged, "Please tell him I'm here. Please."

"Magnus daena want tae ken this about ye, Kaitlyn. He isna interested in hearing that ye are naked and have bedded his father. I assure ye." She inhaled deeply and let out a burst. "And ye are scarred on your face. He winna want tae see it. Tis verra complicated tae find ye here."

"Please. Just tell him. Let me talk to him."

"He winna want tae speak tae ye, anyway. Tis nae matter tae him. He has taken a lovely young mistress and I daena think he considers ye at all."

I collapsed in a naked ball on the bed and sobbed into the bedding.

She huffed.

After a long moment she said, "You are bleeding on the bedclothes. I will speak with Donnan about letting me return ye tae the Island. This favor though will require a promise from ye that this will end our relationship. I have been journeying, collecting artifacts, building wealth for Magnus's ascension, and I daena want tae keep dealing with the trivial matters of a young woman who will nae take no for an answer. Did Magnus nae leave ye after you lost his child? Tis unseemly tae chase him to his father's house. Though I rather respect your commitment to his fortune."

I wailed, "That's not what this is!"

"Yes, well, as a woman I can see ye are verra much regretting being here. I winna tell Magnus that I have found ye, he has already replaced ye with a more capable woman. I will allow him tae keep the untarnished memory of ye in the long ago past. But if I arrange your safe passage away ye will have tae keep away or I will tell Magnus what I found here, what you have done."

She stormed from the room.

~

I guess it could be called sleeping. It was a lot more like passing out. I had checked the whole room, every surface, every drawer I could access. It had been a fast scrabble and I had been squinting, opening my eyes just barely. Peering around then slamming them shut again. The light made it feel like my retinas were burning.

I couldn't find anything. Nothing for a weapon. The door was locked. The bathroom was bare. A toilet in bidet style. A small hand towel that looked used. The thought made me gag. He had touched it? His stinking filthy raping hands had been on this towel?

Then I collapsed until something woke me. I forced my eyes open to the same blaring terrible painful light. Lady Mairead's voice coming through the walls, "—Do you know who that is?"

A man's voice, probably Donnan's, "Of course I know who it is — she told me when she was begging me to let her go last night." His chuckle sent chills up my spine.

"This is a very dangerous game you're playing. Let me take her away. I'll take her to Florida, leave her, return with the vessel. Then you'll have them all and I'll be rid of her again."

"Certainly not." His voice had an air of joviality to it. "Mairead, what would you have me do? Return a gift? She was sent to me too perfect to refuse. I think Magnus will be better controlled if faced with the woman from his past."

"I don't even think he misses her. I think you're mistaken on this."

"Doesn't matter if he wants her or not, he won't want me to have her. He won't like how I've cut her pretty face. And I need him to be ready to fight. My brother, Samuel, has decided to kill him in the arena. Samuel is very lethal. He has never lost a battle."

"You should let Magnus heal first—"

"Don't tell me my business, Mairead. I will not stand for more interference. You mean to advise me? I am the king, how dare you — and what are you?"

His question was met with silence.

"Exactly. You are only Magnus's mother, nothing more. I let you live here because you fill my coffers."

"He will kill you."

"He is imprisoned. He kills who I tell him to kill. My enemies lie dead at his feet. He kneels at mine. If Magnus dies, I'll make the man who killed him kneel, and I will mourn for Magnus only for the amount of time it takes for that to happen."

"So she will stay here in your rooms during your Gala?"

"Oh no Mairead, she will join me. Magnus will be there with his mistress. Samuel will be there, hoping to kill him. Would you like to be there, Mairead, to watch the fun?"

I sat up in bed in a complete fucking panic. I picked up the sheet that was the bottom layer of the bedding and felt along the edge for a good spot. Then I ripped, right down the middle. It ripped clean and easily until it reached the center. I stood up in the middle of the bed, adjusted my hold, and ripped it cleanly all the way to the end where it hitched for a moment. I yanked it clean through. I took the top half of the sheet and stuffed the ripped edge under the rest of the bedding to conceal it. *Come on come on come on, he could walk in any moment.* I stuffed the strip I had torn free under the bedding in a ball.

I laid down and listened. Anything? No noise? Nobody coming?

I pulled the bedding over my arms to cover what I was doing and tied knots on the ends and twisted the torn sheet for the full length of it until it was rope, not great rope, but rope all the same.

Then I sat there with heaving breaths and considered whether I had the strength to strangle a man — and what would be the best position?

I wanted something sharp. Needed something sharp. I jumped from the bed and listened at the door again. Every sound was too loud, buzzing, beeping, roaring noise from every quarter, but no voices, not near, not loud. I grabbed my hastily made rope and wound it around my fist while I entered the bathroom. I climbed up onto the counter on my knees with the full length of my naked body in the mirror, leaned against it, drew back my fist at waist height, and punched — crack! — a crack spread across the width of it. There was also a slice on my fourth knuckle that wasn't bleeding, oh wait, yep, bleeding. But the mirror was now a shattered web of shards. I peeled one away. It was about four inches with a nice long angle. Sort of like a knife with enough of a base to catch in the fabric.

The mirror was trashed. If Donnan went into the bathroom before he came to the bed I would be a dead woman.

I jumped down from the counter and ran to the bed. Under the covers using only my fingers, I created a knot about midway down my rope, shoving the shard into the loop of it, and tied the knot twice around it.

I balled the rope up to the side, with a tail near my fingers so I could find it in a struggle.

Then I lay in the room and waited for Donnan to come to me.

MAGNUS

Bella and I were dressed for the occasion. She looked verra beautiful. Her dress wrapped her body in a blue color that was my favorite. It exposed much of her skin. My mind went tae Kaitlyn and what she would look like in it, but I forced the image away. Ever since I had taken Bella I was tryin' nae tae think on Kaitlyn. Not here. This world was too far removed and too awful to bring her intae it.

I couldna dream of being with Kaitlyn while I was imprisoned and killing men for entertainment. I couldna dream of being worthy of Kaitlyn when I had lain with another woman. I couldna. Twas nae up tae me tae dream on her. I had tae get home and then I had tae beg for her forgiveness.

Bella stood with a long leg exposed and I strapped the gun to her inner thigh. When the folds of fabric fell across her lap they covered it, shimmering and shifting. I hoped that be enough tae hide the weapon.

Bella was quiet.

She said, "Donnan has a way of — he's very wicked. You will

stick to the plan, right, My Magnus, no matter what? Even if you're upset?"

"Och aye, I will stick to the plan. What would I be upset about?"

"I don't know, rumors have it he — I don't know, but don't let him distract you."

The guards came and I was made tae stand and have my body checked for weapons, but she was nae checked at all.

We were led down the long hallways past the rooms. I counted again, but my memory of it was perfect. Once I killed him I would find my way to Donnan's rooms. I would find a vessel and I would go tae Florida. I would get Kaitlyn and we would go tae the past. It was the only place tae hide. I just had tae get through this night.

When we came to the doors of the Great Hall on the ground floor there was a great cacophony of voices inside.

Bella asked, "Has Donnan arrived yet?"

A guard answered her, "He has been delayed in his apartment."

"Oh, he's privately entertaining," Bella said. The doors on the Great Hall opened before us.

KAITLYN

*D*onnan stood and appraised me, a lump under the covers, everything covered but my eyes. I squinted. I wanted to lay there and be 'easy' but the idea of him touching me made my stomach turn. I scrambled to sitting on the pillows, leaned on the headboard, as far away as I could get.

"You'll be attending me tonight at a dinner I have. I brought a dress for you, but now that I've seen you again, I'm of a mind to have some more of you."

I clamped my eyes closed and reminded myself to breathe.

The sounds of him undressing echoed in my ears. My mind raced, could I, would I? Under the covers the loop of rope was in my grip. Could I?

I had to be blank.

I had to leave my body.

I had to let his filthy disgusting hands reach under the covers for my ankles and pull me down the bed.

I had to turn my head while his grotesque breath sounded in my ear and the monstrous weight of him settled on my body pushing me down, down, heavy down. He was big. He would fight me if I did it now. I had to wait until he was distracted by the moment until he was into me completely. So I kept my eyes closed while his shoulder blocked my view of the escape and went rigid when his hand grasped my skin and I waited for terrible long moments while he used me for his goddamn enjoyment and — fuck this guy.

I whispered, "Let's change positions, Donnan."

My words shocked him. His eyes had that glazed look. His disgusting brow was sweaty. His hands were gross. He rose up to let me get up. I pushed him to his side, grabbed the rope as he lowered to the mattress and tossed the loop of it around his neck.

I wanted to be behind him, but I ended up on a side within aim of his right hand, but I yanked the rope anyway because I had to. I had to do it. There was no going back now. I closed the gap on the back of his neck as the realization of what I had done hit him full force. He elbowed me hard, but I held on. "Fuck you fuck you fuck you fuck you." I twisted the ropes twisting my arms as well and held on. He lowered, his hands grasping at the rope, so I jumped to standing using the bounce of the mattress to give me enough force to get the rope twisted, tighter and tighter. "Fuck you! Fuck YOU!!!!"

His arms flailed and fought. His hand found my ankle and pulled me down. I landed on top of him, "Fuck you!" and forced myself back up and twisted more. "Fuck you, I hate you. I hate you! I hate you!"

His hand flailed up and grabbed a wad of my hair and yanked, but I fucking held on. I held on, screeching, wanting to let go and be done with it, but I knew he died or I died. Someone in this fucking room was going to die and it wasn't going to be me. "I hate you!"

He bucked his back slamming me to the mattress, landing on me, ploughing his elbow into my side, but he was weaker now and my arms were closer to my chest giving me more strength. I pulled tighter and twisted more and opened my eyes enough to see the glass shard, useless right beside his throat, jabbed into a knot but not doing anything. He flailed for my hair again.

He was weaker still but also more desperate. His elbow hit me in the ribs knocking my breath, but I held on as he bucked against me. My elbows on his shoulders, my knees around his back. "Stop it! Stop it! Stop it, fuck you, I hate you, I hate you. Fuck. You!"

I put both ends of the rope into my left hand and grasped the edge of the glass and shoved it into his neck. I screeched so loud I hurt my ears. A gush of blood covered us both and repulsed me so much I almost leapt away.

My hatred, my fury made me hold tighter. "I hate you. I hate you." I held the rope in both hands again and tightened it even more. "I hate you. I hate you. I hate you. I hate you."

His arms stopped flailing and his hands went to his neck, trying to pull away the rope, or the shard or both or anything, and that's when I began to cry. I begged, "I'm sorry, I'm so sorry, oh my god I'm sorry," while I held on, waiting for him to die, feeling the life drain from him, skin to skin. I begged the universe for it to happen fast. And begged God for forgiveness for doing it. "I'm sorry. I'm so sorry."

After long long moments I let go. The weight of him was on me and I shoved him off. I was covered in blood and I couldn't stop screaming.

MAGNUS

The Great Hall was packed. I hadn't considered how many people I would need tae speak tae. All eyes turned tae me as I walked in. I glanced at Bella and she was smiling widely.

She began tae introduce me. "Magnus, this is Governor Georges. He's been with Donnan for many years."

I shook his hand. "Magnus, a pleasure. You are the spitting image of your father. He must be very proud. Your fighting in the arena has been spectacular. Well done!"

"Thank you, Governor Georges."

I was introduced to another man. "Magnus, this is the war minister, Donahue."

"Nice tae meet ye, Minister Donahue."

Minister Donahue laughed. "Ye! He said, 'ye!' What do 'ye' think Margaret, are 'ye' all hot and bothered by the young prince?"

The woman beside him twittered and blushed and demurely put out a hand for me to kiss.

Her husband winked. "I'm on your side, Magnus. My wife wouldn't let me pick anyone else." She blushed even more.

One by one I was introduced to a room full of people while Bella kept her hand under my elbow, whispering in my ear, announcin' with her actions that we were together.

Towards the end of the introductions people began tae wonder at the lateness of Donnan. I asked, "What's keeping him do you think?"

There was something in Bella's eyes — she glanced at the doorway at the end of the room. "It's nothing for you to worry about. Just keep to the plan."

I asked, "Is that the stairwell up tae Donnan's apartment?"

She shook her head and looked away, but I already had the answer tae it.

Lady Mairead came over a moment later. "Bella." She nodded curtly. "Magnus, are ye healing well? You daena look verra vigorous; I think ye may need tae lie down. You have met most everyone. I can—"

Bella said, "He doesn't need to lie down. He hasn't met everyone yet, there is his uncle, Samuel. Let me introduce you."

As Bella waved for his attention, Lady Mairead said, "Magnus, be careful of him. He wants the throne and has declared his intention tae go through ye tae get it."

I took a breath.

She shook her head. "Try tae look menacing or he may take his chance right now." Then she immediately said, "Ah Samuel, so good of you tae be here at Donnan's Gala."

The big man standin' in front of me eyed me with much more menace than I could conjure in my weakened state.

Bella interrupted, "Magnus meet—"

Lady Mairead interrupted her. "Samuel, I would like ye tae meet your nephew, Donnan's son, the next in line for the throne, Magnus—"

Uncle Samuel said, "Yeah, yeah, Magnus Archie Colin Campbly, I get it. You've been raised to think you're a king." His chuckle was still more menacing. People around us stopped talking tae listen.

I said, with as much charm as I could manage, "Until verra recently, Uncle, I dinna ken I was a future king, but I have taken tae the idea and for some of us it comes quite natural."

Lady Mairead said, "Magnus, careful."

"You won't be king. Where is Donnan anyway?"

Lady Mairead said, "He's busy."

"It's like him to make us wait. I've asked to fight you tomorrow, Magnus, best be ready."

I projected my voice for the surrounding crowd. "I am always ready tae fight for my rightful place. Yet I wonder at your commitment? Have ye been fighting for the throne, challengin' the other sons of Donnan? Did ye challenge your brother, Tanrick?"

"No, I didn't challenge Tanrick."

"Och, you challenged me without the trial of killin' tae get tae me. I am the next king by birthright, why must I fight ye? I could say ye are beneath me, untested, unproven — it would sully my reputation tae fight ye." Samuel looked furious.

I continued, "I am the future king, but if ye challenge me, am I suppose tae let ye set the terms?" I looked around at the crowd for their approval. "I believe I am busy on the morrow. I have an appointment with my tailor tae let out the front of my kilt." I stood taller and glared at him. "Tis constrictin' tae my broadsword."

The people around us laughed at my joke as the two of us stared into each other's eyes, breathing heavy, locked, a step closer tae battle when the war minister stepped between us. "Samuel. Magnus. Hold it for the arena."

I raised my brow and grinned at him. "Minister Donahue, I

winna fight him tomorrow, but I would fight him later in the month."

"I will set the date in the books." He turned away tae converse with his wife.

Samuel stood close tae me, his chest bowed. "You got away with it this time, Nephew, but you'll still be dead by next week."

"Och, nae by your hands. I imagine much greater men wish me dead. I will spend my time worryin' on them if I worry at all."

He walked away by a few feet and pretended tae nae care about me.

Lady Mairead said, "Watch him Magnus, he is deadly. We have come too far tae watch him take the throne."

"If he kills me I winna be the one watchin' would I? Twould be you. Daena you mean ye have come too far? Seems tae me ye haena one bit of consideration about my life, only the outcome for you."

"Remember, I told ye tae go to your rooms tonight. I told ye tae rest. I warned ye. But whatever happens here this evening, you have made a vow, you arna finished with it."

"What are ye...?"

She pushed away through the crowd.

KAITLYN

*I*t was as if I was floating above the lost little body of a young girl, a stranger, forlorn and crying, but I was untethered, drifting, distant. I couldn't help. I wanted to wash her. To give her some clothes. Help her dress. Hold her while she cried, but I couldn't do anything but cover my ears and clamp my eyes shut and beg for forgiveness.

And when I opened my eyes to watch the young girl below she was struggling, and screaming. It was terrifyingly loud and breathtakingly long and soul-shatteringly forlorn. She was shaking so much I thought she might fall apart into pieces on the rug of the blood-splattered room.

She stood and pushed the hair from her eyes, smearing blood across her cheek, and with trembling hands she pulled the dress from the hanger, stepped into it, and pulled the slithery fabric up and tried to twist it to make sense of its placement. A filmy fabric stretched across her breasts, formed in the wrong places, loose in the others. It barely mattered because once up she caught sight of the body again. She screamed, like she had forgotten, but there it was —

She screamed more, her voice burned ragged from the strain of it.

She found the key to the door in the pants of the dead man and unlocked her prison.

The trance broke. She flung her body out the door, collapsed on the ground, struggled back up, and I was able to pull myself down to meet her, to pick her up, and beg her to run, run Kaitlyn, run away. He can't hurt you anymore.

MAGNUS

Bella pressed against me. "That was awesome My Magnus. I adore you when you are aggressive like that. It makes me want you even more."

I cut my eyes at her. "I want the gun."

"Not until dinner, under the table. They might search you. That's when—"

"I want it now. Uncle Samuel intends tae kill me and he has a weapon on him. I could tell in his eyes when he was threatenin' me."

She said, "I don't know how I will give it to you here in a crowded—'

I pushed her up against the wall, pulled up the front of her skirt, and wrestled the gun free from her thigh holster. I released her. "Thank ye."

I shoved the gun intae my belt and ran my fingers through my hair while she struggled tae put her dress back tae rights. I chuckled and took a swig of the glass of wine she asked me tae hold. Then I heard someone screamin'.

MAGNUS

*T*he screamin' was coming from the far side of the room. I pushed Bella protectively behind me and tried tae make sense of the sound as it echoed around the Great Hall.

I glanced over my shoulder at Bella — she was wide-eyed, scared. The sound went on, a wail of despair and fear, and it was echoin', fillin', shockin' my ears.

Every person turned toward that end of the room.

Bella grabbed my arm and pleaded, "Magnus, let the guards take you to your room, please, it's not safe for you, please."

"What dost ye mean?" The screaming continued. I yanked free of Bella's grip and began tae push my way through the crowds. "Excuse me. Excuse me. Pardon me."

A woman at the far end of the crowded room was pleading — "Help me please, please someone, please help me."

The rest of the hall was quiet, people backed away, bumpin' intae me, making it hard tae get through the crowd tae see—

Kaitlyn

—covered in blood, wringin' her hands and beggin' for help. I pushed through and rushed tae where she stood. "Kaitlyn!" She was overwrought, her hair knotted and matted, blood everywhere, a jagged cut down her cheek, shakin', barely clothed, but the most frightenin' of all — she dinna see me.

Her eyes were open but she was starin' at the air, holdin' her bloodied hands before her, beggin' us tae take pity on her, blank as if what she had seen — what frightened her this much, was still there — a ghost was terrifyin' her.

I grasped her bloody forearms and tried tae see into her eyes. "Kaitlyn, tis me, Magnus. Kaitlyn!" I shook her tryin' tae get through the fog of her mind. "Kaitlyn what are ye—"

Her wail was long and piteous.

"Kaitlyn when did ye — what happened? Ye are covered in blood."

She sobbed, "I killed him." Her eyes were wild, left and right, not focusin'.

"Who, who did you kill?"

"I killed Donnan." The room erupted into mayhem behind me.

The crowd was closin' in. I pulled her behind me and held ontae her with an arm. She clutched at my shirt but I dinna think she kent twas me.

A man's voice said, "Guards arrest her." I searched for the place it emanated from but found nobody tae argue with. The guards were advancing.

I spoke tae the crowd. "I need tae check Donnan's rooms."

Uncle Samuel stepped forward. "Give us the woman, Magnus. She has committed murder."

I put up a stayin' hand and tried tae sound imperious. "We daena ken, we daena ken what happened. We canna—"

Samuel pressed toward me. "Release her, Magnus, turn her over to the guards."

"I winna. I am the heir of Donnan. I am the next king. This is my wife and I winna turn her over."

Samuel stepped toward me, his hands out placatingly. "Magnus, calm down — your wife? You can see this will need to be investigated."

I yelled, "Minister Donahue!" The war minister stepped forward from the crowd. "What is the protocol? I am the next king am I not? I order the—"

Samuel stepped forward again, closer, making tae grab for Kaitlyn. "You may be the son of Donnan, but I am his brother. You're protecting his murderer. We will need to determine the true next-in-line."

I pulled my gun and aimed it at him. Guests gasped and stepped back.

Without takin' my eyes from him, I asked again, "Minister Donahue, am I not the next in line for the throne? And as such, tis within my rights tae tell the guard tae step back. I order ye, Uncle, take three steps back. There may come a day when ye fight for my throne, but today is nae the day." Samuel put his hands up but stepped back into the crowd.

I waved the gun around the room. "Anyone want tae argue with me about my rightful throne?"

Kaitlyn was sinkin' behind me, I strengthened my hold on her. "Anyone?" I began walkin' backward tae the door. Kaitlyn clutched my shirt, cowering against me, yet stepping along in time.

I made it tae the door and pushed Kaitlyn through it. Lady Mairead ran up behind. "Go fast tae Donnan's apartments, Magnus. I will meet ye there."

I turned tae see her slip back through the door tae attempt tae calm the crowd. I grasped Kaitlyn around the waist and pulled her up the flights of stairs and down the long hall — a door was open, light spillin' out, a handprint of blood smeared across the open door. I pulled tae a stop—

A stark room, a bed, Donnan naked on his back, dead in the middle of it. Everywhere a struggle. Blood all over.

Kaitlyn covered her mouth to stifle her cry. I wanted tae join her. The room told me the full story and hearin' it made me want tae kill him anew.

I enfolded her under an arm and hustled her down the hall tryin' the next door and the next. The last opened ontae an office. With a glance I saw my sword and its sheath across the desk. "Kaitlyn, stand here." I crossed tae the desk for the sword.

I pushed the gun intae my belt at my waist.

Kaitlyn had gone thankfully quiet on the matter so I could think better.

Lady Mairead stormed in. "Kaitlyn has killed him. This is very complicated."

I crossed tae stand in front of Kaitlyn again. I finished buckling the strap on my chest. "I ken."

"And you didn't kill Samuel. You should have when you had the chance."

I asked, "Tell me, did ye ken Kaitlyn was here?"

She looked shocked. "What?"

"Did ye ken she was here, Lady Mairead, did ye?" I looked wildly around for one of the vessels.

"If ye must hear it, Bella told me. I was trying tae convince Donnan tae let me take her home."

I stopped looking for the vessel. Fury beat my chest with fast breaths. "Bella told ye that Kaitlyn was here?"

"Yes, she saw Kaitlyn here. We were trying tae get her out before—"

"Before I found out, and ye were tryin' tae get me tae go tae my room tonight. What would have happened tae her—" A cough broke my words. My ribs hurt so much I wanted tae fall tae the floor. I gasped for breath.

She said, "I wanted ye tae go tae your room because ye are nae well. You're blue Magnus, you're wheezing, and the doctors should see tae ye. I will take Kaitlyn tae Florida. Ye can stay here—"

"You winna touch her. I want all the vessels."

She shook her head.

"Give them tae me now or I will kill ye tae get it."

She pulled a vessel from a pocket within her dress. "'Tis the only one I have and I hardly think this necessary tae—"

"'Tis necessary. The fact that I haena killed ye yet is surprisin' me. I have been verra merciful, but daena push me. I want all the other vessels. Where did Donnan keep them?"

"If ye are leaving, ye need tae go fast."

"Give me the vessels!" I held my ribs riding a wave of pain.

She went to the desk, used a key tae unlock it, and pilfered through a drawer. "He kept one here, the rest are locked up in his vault. It will take too long tae get tae them."

She handed me the second vessel. "You need tae be out of this castle tae travel. The place where I journey from is through a tunnel but it's a long distance. Go fast, I will hold them off. Go tae Florida, see a doctor. Minister Donahue and Governor Georges and I will do our best tae hold the kingdom. But I think Samuel has an army of men who will be looking for ye. Go."

I nodded and put the vessels in my sporran.

"Kaitlyn, can ye run?"

MAGNUS

I ran down six flights of stairs tae the tunnel entrance, an arm around Kaitlyn, lifting her, draggin' her sometimes. I couldna speak. I could barely breathe, but when I looked back at her face, she was cryin' and was lost tae me. She stumbled tae the ground. I pulled her up by an arm and she saw her hands again and began tae cry at the sight. Her sobs echoed on the walls of the tunnel, comin' at me from all directions. I pulled her tae standin' and forced her tae run.

Men were comin' along the passage behind us and I feared I couldna run fast enough. We turned corners but men were close behind. We were nearin' the end though. The tunnel here was stacked full of Donnan's plunder, filling the edges of the floor, leanin' against the walls, and jutting into our path. I was beginning tae stagger. I shoved a marble statue so it fell across the hallway. I tossed a painting on top. I pulled a rolled tapestry and tossed it across that. Twould nae hold them for long.

A few more feet and I shoved another sculpture over and another. It barely slowed the men down. We came tae the door at the end and shoved through it tae a wide rock ledge juttin' over a rushing river.

I slammed the door shut behind us and pulled Kaitlyn toward the edge. I coughed and held an arm across my ribs tryin' tae bear the pain. "We are leavin' Kaitlyn, I have ye, we are together. Daena be afraid." I pulled her close tae my wheezing chest, pulled one of the vessels from my sporran, twisted it, and coughed so that I almost doubled over. I recovered just enough tae say the numbers. The storm built above us as the men were comin' through the door.

PART II
KAITLYN

CHAPTER 37

*S*omething moved near my head. I pulled myself up from the trauma and pain of the journey. I didn't know where I was or how I had gotten here. I only knew that the shit hurt on every level. My skin. My core. My every single hair. It's how I knew I had journeyed — the intense all-consuming pain. Because my mind was blank on everything.

I submerged under another wave of agony and curled on my side, my hands tucked under my chin — oh my god, oh my god, oh my god — blood was all over my hands.

I killed him. The blood. My breath was fast — what the fuck? I was covered in blood.

I startled — a hand beside me shifted.

Magnus.

I looked up at his face. I wiggled nearer him and burst into tears. "I killed him. Oh god I killed him — I killed him." I sobbed into my blood-covered hands.

Magnus's eyes opened barely, his voice was very low and strained. "Aye. Ye have killed him Kaitlyn, but I — I daena feel verra well. Can ye take the gun in your hand and watch the sky?"

He coughed and wheezed for a long time. Groaning and holding his ribs.

"Are you okay?" I pulled the gun from his belt.

"Can ye walk yet?"

"I don't think so."

"Then I just need tae rest. If ye would watch for them twould help."

I laid my head on his thigh, the gun on my chest, staring up at the sky trying to stay on top of the waves of pain.

I woke a while later. I was barely dressed and it was cool, not freezing, but too cold to be wearing, I looked down at my outfit, a freaking strip of cloth. And I had blood everywhere.

I would need to deal with a lot of shit when I could think about it. I was on the forest floor of a — where the hell was I? I looked up, the trees, the ground, the big rock — I was in Scotland. When in Scotland? Magnus's eyes were clamped tight, his lips a bit blue on the edges. "Magnus?"

"Och." His eyes remained closed.

"What year are we, can I go get Quentin?"

Magnus groaned and said, "1703."

"Can you move now?"

"I canna, Kaitlyn. I think ye should run tae Balloch, ask Sean tae come get me. Bring men."

"Oh," I looked around the wooded area we were in. This was a lot for me to figure out. "Magnus, where is Balloch? What direction?"

His finger pointed. "Tell Sean..." he moaned, "southwest near the river. Go fast."

"Shit, shit, shit, shit." I ran. I ran as fast as I could in as straight a line as I could, and it wasn't long before the woods cleared and there was a field and beyond it men near the familiar gates of Balloch. "Help! Help! Sean Campbell, I need Sean Campbell, Lizbeth—" I was winded and possibly insane looking, covered in dried blood, barely dressed, and the clothes I barely wore were seriously foreign.

The men gawked, and I didn't recognize any of them. "It's Magnus, Magnus Campbell, he's injured." I pointed towards the woods, "Magnus! Magnus Campbell! Tell the Earl!"

One of the men left for the castle. The other men leered at me while I pleaded with the universe, "Hurry please. Magnus is injured."

After a few long moments, Sean and Lizbeth rushed out through the castle gates. Sean asked, "What happened, Madame Kaitlyn?"

"Magnus is injured, he's really — he's sick, back there, through the trees," I gestured the way I had come, "southwest, the river."

Lizbeth asked, "Tis Magnus's blood? What happened?"

"No, he — he can't breathe, it's not his," I gestured breathing in and out, though I could barely do it either.

Sean was already gathering men and sending messages into the castle and to the stables and then he was gone, with six men, seven horses, before I could believe it was possible.

Lizbeth wanted me to get dressed. She murmured sweet-nesses over the cut on my cheek. She bustled me into the castle though I wanted to stand and stare at the woods until I saw Magnus coming. But Lizbeth led me to the laundry room where an older woman wiped me down with a cloth dipped in a bucket of water and then with the filthy blood water they cleaned the cut on my face. Watching the red water roll down my skin made me begin to cry anew and I wondered if I would ever be able to stop.

Lizbeth asked, "Were ye attacked, Kaitlyn?"

I nodded crying.

"Tis a shame, we haena seen ye in months and now this. Whenever ye leave I worry on ye so much. Tis much like trouble follows Young Magnus. He gets in more than most and drags ye intae it."

She spoke to the woman washing me and I was brought a white shift to wear. The women were fascinated by my dress. It looked like water the way it shimmered and flowed and felt like silk. Lizbeth was admiring it so much I gave it to her, happy for it not to be mine anymore.

And then Lizbeth adjusted the tartan around her shoulders and it dawned on me to ask, "You're pregnant?"

"Aye, I be with child, Kaitlyn. I haena seen ye in many months." She whispered, "I landed the husband I was wantin' too." She loaned me a plain bodice and a dark skirt and helped me step into it. She was lacing up the back when one of the women entered to give us news. "They have Young Magnus in the upper rooms now. He daena look well."

I burst into tears again. "I need to go see him."

"Of course." Lizbeth gave my laces a last tug and tied them. "I'll send for the physician."

One of the young women led me up the back stairs to our room.

Sean was standing outside the door. When I arrived he asked, "Is Lizbeth sending for the physician?"

"Yes." His face was so worried I thought I might faint.

He asked quietly, "What happened tae him?"

"I don't know, broken ribs?" I clutched my skirts in my hands. "Do you think he's going to be okay?"

He scowled, "The physician will come, although he heals verra few."

I couldn't say anything else. I rushed to Magnus's bed and climbed in beside him. He was staring up at the ceiling. I nuzzled my face onto his shoulder. "What should I do?"

He said, "I likely need tae rest, the physician told me such before and I hadna time."

"Were your lips blue like this when you saw the doctor? Because you don't look—"

He shook his head. He gasped for a breath. "He was givin' me air."

"Oh." I tried to imagine why we ended up here in the eighteenth century. "Why didn't we go to Florida?"

"Because Lady Mairead—" He coughed, groaned, and held his ribs.

I said, "You need pain medicine too. Plus air." I crawled off the bed. "I'm going to go get it for you."

"Nae Kaitlyn."

I opened his sporran and pulled out a vessel. Then I walked his sporran with the other vessel to the other end of the room as far away from the bed as I could get it. "Don't you follow me, Magnus. I'm going for medicine."

"Ye canna travel—"

"I can and I will."

"What if they grab ye while you are..."

His gun was in the sporran too. "I'm taking the gun. And what if? But you know what, fuck them. Fuck all of them. I'm going to get you some medicine." I turned to the bed. "Don't you die. Do you understand me? Don't die. Just lie here and breathe and don't die. I mean it."

I ran out the door. When I passed Lizbeth in the hall, I said, "I forgot something. I have to go get it," too frantic to come up with any plausible excuses.

"I should come with you—"

"I'll be back! Wait, what day is it today?"

"Four days before Lughnasadh."

I pulled to a stop. "Lunessa?"

"Aye, in four days we will celebrate Lughnasadh, the harvest festival."

I had no idea what that meant. But just to be clear I asked, "Lunessa is a day in 1703?"

"Och aye, but maybe ye think of it as Lammas? Are ye feeling well, Kaitlyn?"

"Not really, but I really have to go get something. Will you watch over Magnus? Don't let the physician do anything crazy to him."

"Like what?"

I started running again. "I don't know, like bloodletting or something — no leeches!" I ran down the hall, out the door, across the courtyard, through the gates, over the gravel drive, across the field, and into the woods as far as I thought I needed to go. I was thinking the whole way, *when did I leave, when should I get back? What date? Lunessa, Lama's day, lama day, llama day?* I counted in my head, picked a date, two weeks after my trip to Scotland, and then I twisted the ends of the vessel and recited the numbers. The ones I knew best, aimed for the beach in front of my old house in Florida. Because I had no idea how to get to the apartment building where I actually lived.

CHAPTER 38

I forced myself awake, clenched my jaw and forced myself up. I'm sure I looked like a monster — matted hair with dried blood, because that hurried sponge bath in the eighteenth century hadn't been good enough. Plus the whole bodice and skirt thing. My expression. I wanted to scream but couldn't. My throat couldn't take it anymore. I was incapable of the screams that needed to come.

Now I needed to save Magnus's life.

The beach was empty, being in the middle of a windstorm. The tide was high and I was super lucky I didn't land in the ocean because it was churning like a washing machine. The wind sandblasted my skin. I lurched over a sand dune and realized I had to walk about five houses down to the public access.

I tucked against the wind and pushed my body toward the path. I'm pretty sure I blacked out for a little while because I remember nothing until I was standing on the edge of the road, waving my arms, hoping a car would pull over for me.

It was someone I knew, Matt Jones, from high school.

Barely functioning I got into the back of his car.

"Um, I'm not an Uber, Katie, but you need a ride? I'll give you a ride."

I gave him my address.

"Man, I haven't seen you in forever. I'm living in Jax now, just up here to see my parents. What you been doing with yourself?" His eyes kept checking me out in the rear-view mirror.

"I got married."

"Anyone I know, not James right?" He shook his head. "He was nothing but trouble."

"Not James, you don't know him. He's from Scotland."

"Oh." He sat for a moment at a red light. "Well, hopefully he treats you better. What's with the costume?"

I clamped my eyes shut. "Costume party, a mean hangover, that's why I'm so..."

"Yeah, I get it, morning after sucks enough, but the costumes make it even worse. You look down and 'Why the hell am I dressed like Batman at nine in the morning?'"

I tried to laugh but didn't really have it in me.

A few minutes later he left me in the lot in front of my door and Quentin was rushing from the apartment to meet me.

CHAPTER 39

I could barely get the words out because they tumbled out of me all at once. "I found him, he's sick, oh my god, I came for medicine—"

Quentin asked, "Where is he? And why are you — Katie there's blood all around your hairline," he picked up my hand, "your fingernails. What happened?"

Zach and Emma rushed over from their place. Zach said, "What the fuck happened? Are you okay?"

"No, not really. I went to the future. I found Magnus. It was not good. I killed someone, Donnan, his dad really. I killed him."

"Holy shit Katie, keep your voice down," Quentin put an arm around me and brought me into the apartment and closed and locked the door behind me. "Okay, what happened again? How did you get the cut on your face?"

I wailed, "I don't have time to tell you all the details. Magnus is really sick, but I went to the future and I was a captive and this man was all over me, raping me. He cut me, and I—"

I sobbed into my hands.

"—and I killed him. But then I just murdered the king so they wanted to arrest me and Magnus got me out of there and took me to Scotland. I think he thought we would be safer there." My eyes got wide. "Has anyone been here, anyone looking for us, me?"

Quentin said, "No, no one."

"After we time jumped to Scotland, I woke up and Magnus is not well. His lips are blue, he's having trouble breathing. He's in a castle and—"

Quentin said, "Shit Katie, what is it, what's wrong with him?"

"I don't know, I think a broken rib?"

Emma said, "My dad broke a rib once in a car accident. He punctured a lung, and it hurt really bad. He had to have oxygen and—"

"Can you Google it for me, what I need? I have to get back to him. I can't stay here. I have to go..." Zach ran next door for his laptop. Quentin was investigating the gun I brought with me.

Emma said, "You really need to take a shower Katie. You're covered in someone's blood. It's dried in your hair and you smell like blood. You have to shower. Zach will Google it. He'll make a list. We'll collect it all and then you can go back. We'll work fast."

"Promise?" I twisted my skirt in my hands. "Promise you'll go fast?"

"I promise."

I started to walk to the shower. "Can you come with me Emma? I don't want to be alone with myself."

"Of course."

When we went to the bathroom I tried to sound normal and not on the edge of a breakdown though who was I kidding? I had tipped over the edge already. I was in breakdown. I just couldn't stop moving and live in breakdown-town because Magnus was going to die— "So where's Ben?"

"He's asleep, you got here right at his naptime." She turned on the shower and adjusted the temperature controls. Then she helped me undo the laces Lizbeth had laced just hours before. Centuries before.

My hands were shaking. It was hard to breathe and that reminded me of Magnus struggling to breathe and here I was in Florida climbing into a hot shower, a murderer.

Emma helped me climb out of my clothes. I got into the stall, closed my eyes and stepped under the water. Then I opened my eyes and looked down —

"I can't— oh no. Oh no oh no oh no. There's blood, every-where, oh no — I killed him. I can't..." I burst into tears and cowered on the wall as far away as I could get from the water. I put my hands to my eyes, but then remembered my hands had blood on them. I tucked them into my armpits and cried piteously.

Through the clear shower walls I saw Emma kick off her leather shoes. The stall door opened and Emma stepped in fully clothed. She made soft shhhhhh noises, took the shower head off the wall, and began to wave it over my hair. "Shhhhhh Katie, it's okay, It's okay."

She ran the water making her soft calming noises until she said, "See, the water is running clear now. Wait, close your eyes again." She concentrated the water on an area near my right ear where I smeared blood right after I killed him. "It's in your ear, hold on, keep them closed."

Then she washed under my hair on the nape of my neck. "You're missing a hunk of hair here."

"He did that."

"And he cut your cheek?"

I nodded.

"Raise your arms." She directed the water all over me. "I need to ask, you've been taking the pill, right? I've been filling your prescription..."

"Yes, I was on it."

"Good."

"Yeah, that would've sucked." I closed my eyes while she spayed around my face. "I'm going to have to give you a raise now that you've had to bathe blood off me." I sort of laughed even though the joke was very weak.

"Working for you is truly insane. Months of barely anything and then something so big and bizarre I wonder if it's ever happened in the history of the world."

"Welcome to my life. All I do is wait for Magnus, then almost die when I'm with him."

She lathered shampoo in her palm and began to wash my hair. "How did you do it?"

"Kill him?" I gulped. "I waited until he was on me and got a rope around his n—" I pantomimed tightening it.

"Fuck Katie."

I laughed through my tears. "You sound like Zach."

"The moment calls for it. That is the scariest thing I've ever heard. I'm amazed you survived it." She rinsed me on all sides. "You know, Hayley is right about you, you're a freaking super-hero." She handed me some soap. "Lather up all your underparts. Get that creep off you good."

I did as I was told. I was bundled into towels and herded into a bathrobe. And though I begged her to let me get ready to go and go already, Emma bossily replied that I should eat something, let them gather my stuff, and then I could go.

Quentin and Zach were gone — headed to the medical supply store, the drug store, and the grocery store.

Emma went next door to check on Ben and grab me some food. I couldn't remember the last time I ate. At least a day. Maybe longer. While she was gone, I sat in silence and stared at my wedding photo on the wall.

I didn't recognize myself in it.

I looked young and carefree. But also, at the time, terrified, but that brand of terror — scared of Magnus? Seemed so pedestrian now.

Emma returned with Ben in the sling. I drank glass after glass of ice water. Then asked for a beer. The pain of the journey was almost abated. I was at the stage now where I could usually begin to think about getting up. Mind over matter. I would need to remember that I was capable of it when I got back to Scotland today. I would get up. I would save Magnus's life.

Quentin and Zach brought up bags and bags of stuff and then they sat down on chairs and acted like they had a big thing to say.

"What?"

Quentin said, "This time I'm for real going with you."

"No, it's gotten more dangerous than I—"

He interrupted, "How long have I been working for Magnus?"

"Like two years."

"Yep. And I think I've done a good job. I've kept you safe while you're here. Have you had any near-death experiences while I've been your security guard?"

"No."

"But you guys won't let me really guard you. You won't let me journey with you. In Scotland you went by yourself and look what happened, I couldn't protect you when you need me. So here's the thing, I'm going with you today or I'm resigning and you'll have to find someone else to watch this empty apartment because I'm done with guarding Zach. Nothing ever happens around him."

"But—"

Zach said, "I agree Katie. He's going with you. I'll send a sack of food and he'll attend you—"

"You can't, Quentin. You don't know how awful it is. It hurts. Emma, do you hear this?"

Emma said, "Yep, I hear him, and I agree with him, Katie. He should go with you."

"But it's even deadlier now."

Zach asked, "Where is Magnus right now?"

"A castle."

"With his family around him, a fucking castle. Probably with a moat."

"No moat."

"Okay, that doesn't matter, no moat, fine. But he's got his family there, weapons, and though it's been dangerous, he hasn't let anything happen to you. He'll keep Quentin safe. Quentin will keep you guys safe. Plus, a while back I bought astronaut ice cream for him and he needs it. Quentin will deliver it. I bought a ton of food. I'm going to load it up and Quentin will carry it in the cooler. Quentin will take guns."

"I don't know."

"I'm not comfortable working for you guys anymore if you won't listen to us about doing what is safest, right? Emma and I both. I'll end up working at McDonalds and raising Baby Ben on minimum wage."

I kept staring at Quentin blinking. I was going to take him before, but now... This decision was beyond me. It felt life and death, but also he was being so serious about it, like he wouldn't work for me anymore. I needed to ask Magnus if it was okay, but I couldn't, and time was running out. "What if Magnus doesn't make it?"

Zach and Quentin didn't answer, but Emma said, "Even more of a reason for him to go. To help you come home. I think you should let him help you."

A memory flashed, my bloodied hands, my voice, *Help me, please... please, help me.*

"Okay, you can come. Just to help me get Magnus well. Then he decides what to do with you. You'll need clothes, maybe

Magnus's kilts?" I tried to think if I was forgetting anything. "Oh, can someone figure out what Lunessa Llama day is? I left four days before Llama feast day."

~

Forty-five minutes later I was back in my dress. Quentin was wearing one of Magnus's traditional kilts in black with a modern gun in a holster belted around his waist. Plus a loose black shirt with a shoulder holster and another gun. Also a sword. A cloak to hide it all. He was wearing a pair of hiking boots. A bag containing a three thousand dollar portable oxygen concentrator was slung over his shoulder. In the side pockets of the bag we stuffed five very expensive extra batteries.

He also carried a soft-sided cooler with the astronaut ice cream, antibiotics, pain killers, protein shake powder, Emergen-C packets, yogurt in tubes, and a lot of food. Emma filled a ziploc bag with a bunch of hippy meds — rescue remedy, essential oils, arnica, and some herbs.

And we were off.

I knew now that Lughnasadh was a harvest festival that was celebrated on August 1 in 1703. And we figured out what numbers to say to return on the date four days before.

The weather was whipping — wet, windy, insane. We said goodbye to Zach and Emma and Baby Ben in the car and then they sat with the window wipers running and the lights on while we fought the winds to get out to the beach.

"It's really painful. I'm truly sorry about this."

Quentin said, "Just do it already, I saw combat action, I got it." We huddled together and held on to each other's forearms.

I twisted the vessel and said the numbers for Balloch Castle and ripped a friend out of time with me.

CHAPTER 40

I was in the dirt writhing and moaning in pain. My voice inside — getupgetupgetupgetup — I forced myself to sit. I shook Quentin, "How are you doing?"

"Ugh." He writhed deeper into the muck of the forest floor.

"Are you okay?"

He groaned.

"I have to go, go to the castle and I need you to come with me. I can't leave you here." I waited for a moment, then jiggled him again. "Get up. I know it hurts but get up."

Quentin pulled himself to a sitting position and put his head in his hands.

"Here's the thing. I'm going to start kicking you. I'm glad you're here, but you have to get up get up get up."

Quentin joked, "Sheesh Katie, getting all worked up."

"Magnus, Quentin. Magnus needs us, get up."

Quentin said, "Is it dark for you? Is your breathing super loud?"

"Totally, you have to get up anyway."

He stirred and then got up and we gathered our stuff. "You weren't wrong, this hurts like shit."

"Yep. Now you get to run through the woods to a castle in the eighteenth century. This is where it gets weird."

CHAPTER 41

This was where it got really really weird. Lizbeth met us at the front gates and immediately pulled me aside. "You've been gone for hours Kaitlyn, who is this man?" She shot a nervous glance at Quentin.

It dawned on me that we had absolutely no back story

"Um, this is um, Magnus's guard." I glanced at Quentin. He was staring open-mouthed up at the building's facade. "He was coming to meet me and I only just remembered it, just when..." My voice trailed off. She and the other men were staring at him.

Quentin looked nervous, shifting and looking around.

"His name is Quentin Peters. He's um, a friend of my father's from the West Indies. He was assigned to travel with me here, to protect me, but we were separated for a while and um, he works for Magnus."

"He belongs tae Magnus?"

"Oh dear lord, no, um..." I glanced at Quentin. "He works with... I can't think — he's a free man — Magnus thinks of him like family. Can Magnus explain later?"

"He is wearing a kilt?"

"Sure, all the men in the West Indies do. Is Magnus okay?"

She said, "Magnus is the same, I'll see you up tae his room, and then I will explain your black friend tae the Earl."

Walking behind her I stole a glance at Quentin, who mouthed, "What the fuck, they think I'm Magnus's slave?"

I mouthed back, "I'm sorry."

And then we were in Magnus's room. I asked Lizbeth, "Has the physician been here?"

"He left for some tinctures, but has nae applied anythin' yet."

"Can you convince him to stay away? Quentin brought some medicines for him from home."

"I will do my best, but just between us, Kaitlyn, the physician is verra set in his ways, and he won't take kindly tae bein' turned away. But I will tell Sean tae take the matter over."

"Thank you Lizbeth." I hugged her. "I missed you."

"I missed ye too, Kaitlyn. Now go kiss your husband and make him better."

I crossed to his bed. "Magnus?"

He opened his eyes and tried a tiny smile. He was very weak. His lips were tinged that freaky blue, his breathing wheezed. "Hey, I brought a friend for you."

Magnus looked at Quentin but his eyes were unfocused, as if he couldn't tell who he actually was.

Quentin said, "So, Boss, you look like hell, really. That time your face got beat up? This is worse. What happened?" He set up the oxygen concentrator reading the manual to get it started.

I helped him move it to the other side of the bed so it would be hidden from the door. When it was on it made a crazy-loud whirring noise but there was nothing we could do about that.

I put the mask over Magnus's nose and mouth. He gave me a sad smile.

Quentin said, "After you get a little air we're going to start feeding you with the supplies Zach sent. First, with some vitamins, then a protein shake. And I've got a treat for you, an ice cream..."

Magnus's eyes shot to Quentin's face as if he recognized him for the first time. His brow drew down. He turned to me and pulled at the mask.

I pushed the mask back to his face. "He came because he insisted. He made me bring him. We'll talk about it when you feel better."

He nodded and settled down. Quentin and I got him to sit forward briefly while we built the mattress into a back rest behind him so his lungs were elevated. We gave him pain killers, some vitamins, and a bit of a powder shake and soon he drifted off into a comfortable sleep.

Quentin lurked around the room checking it out and then sat on the settee and we waited for Magnus to wake up hoping he would feel better when he did.

Sean and Lizbeth appeared later and knocked on the door. I met them in the hallway and told them that Magnus was sleeping. They took Quentin to the Great Hall for dinner and promised to show him to his sleeping quarters after. I wished I felt better, that this wasn't so death-defyingly awfully traumatic and I could go watch the spectacle of Quentin eating dinner in the eighteenth century, but I was waiting at Magnus's bedside for him to breathe. I couldn't take a break for a meal, instead I ate a protein bar and a cheese stick from the bag of food Zach sent.

CHAPTER 42

*I*t was very dark when Magnus groaned and swung his legs off the side of the bed. I was laying beside him, curled on my side, with no mattress under me because it was all folded under Magnus's back. I was trying to decide whether I should expend the required effort to adjust the bedding so I could lay on the bear skin or continue to deal with the wood planks.

"Magnus?"

He pulled the mask from his face. "I have tae relieve m'self."

"Oh." I couldn't see anything but dark as my husband shuffled around the bed and pissed into a chamber pot at the side and then shuffled back. He sat down with a groan and put his head in his hands. He picked up one of the bottles of water Zach sent and drank half of it down. He rolled back to the bed again.

He picked up the mask, slid the elastic over his head, and brought the mask down over his nose and mouth.

I asked, "Are you comfortable?" I watched the dark area that was my husband and saw a movement that I took to be a nod.

I turned to my back and lay there for a while listening to the whir of the machine. Tears began to flow down my cheeks pooling in my ears and there wouldn't be a Kleenex for centuries.

"I'm sorry," I said, "I'm so sorry that I made it so dangerous for you. That I interfered." I swiped at my tears with the heel of my hand. "I shouldn't have gone and I pulled you away from your new life there — I thought you were communicating with me. I thought you were sending me a message. That you wanted me to come. I thought you were meeting me. And I was so stupid. I'm so sorry."

Magnus turned his head to look down at me from his almost upright position. He pulled the mask up. "I haena the breath tae speak, mo reul-iuil..." There was a long pause. Then he said, "but..." the next pause was longer still, "I love ye."

I nodded.

I said, "Okay," like that took all the bad that happened away. Like he meant it.

Then I stared up into the darkness flat on my back crying while I thought about all the things I had gotten wrong.

CHAPTER 43

*I*t had grown light in our room. Magnus's hand was over mine. When I looked up he was looking down at me. "Good morn."

"Good morning. Are you feeling better?" I pulled my hand from his.

"Much. I daena feel I need the machine anymore." I sat up and pulled his mask off, powered down the machine, rolled the tubes up, and put it all away. Magnus watched me the whole time. I went around the bed and sorted through the cooler for his medicine and poured some ibuprofen in my hand. "Take these." I passed him the water bottle. "Hungry?"

"Starved." He quickly added, "Am I mistaken, is Master Quentin here?"

"I think so. I brought him or rather our staff forced me to bring him, but I haven't seen him since yesterday when Sean came to take him to dinner."

Magnus chuckled. "I would have verra much liked tae see him in the Great Hall his first time."

"You're smiling, you do feel better."

"The physician told me I needed tae rest. I daena believe runnin' and fightin' and time-journeyin' was the idea of it."

"Yeah..."

There was a knock on the door. I jumped to answer it. Lizbeth, Sean, and Quentin were in the hall. "Just a minute." I jogged to the bed and hid the water bottles and the machine under a blanket.

"Okay!" They all came in and Lizbeth came directly to the bedside. "Young Magnus, are ye well, or shall I send the physician in tae take the life from ye?"

Magnus chuckled. "Nae, I am well enough, daena send the physician his remedies smell like a pig's wind."

Sean said, "Tis good tae see ye better brother." He sat down on the bed. "Your man has had a time in the Great Hall. Twas much drinkin' and carryin' on. I have been told a story of ye, that ye have been often wearin' a pair of trews that are so tight on your caber ye must walk on your tiptoes."

Magnus groaned.

Sean laughed. "Ye canna deny it! And this kilt ye are wearin' brother, tis a woman's?"

Magnus looked down and moaned. "I haena a chance tae properly clothe."

"Your man who is black as night and haena ever seen the Highlands afore is better kilted than ye." He clapped him on a knee. "We have a festival in a few days, ye best be up for it." He and Lizbeth left the room.

I watched this exchange and then everything caught up with me — the fear. The racing through time. The trying-to-save Magnus's life. Murdering a king. I sat on the settee near the hearth with tears welling up. I probably needed a lot more sleep. Like six months worth.

"Are ye all right, Kaitlyn?"

"I think I was running on sheer terror, now I just need to collapse over here."

"Och aye," said Magnus, "ye journeyed three times verra close. Twas heroic."

I nodded, my face hidden in my arms on the back of the settee.

Magnus said to Quentin, "I am rather glad tae see ye, Master Quentin and I hear ye brought food, though by my count ye have been here many hours and I am still hungry as a spring bear."

Quentin laughed. "I brought some food." He dug through the cooler.

Magnus asked, "Ye made it tae the eighteenth century then, what dost ye think of the place?"

"First off, I kinda forgot about the whole slavery thing. I'm not used to being asked if I'm the property of someone. And come to find out I'm the only black man many of them have seen."

"You told them ye were a friend of mine?"

"Katie told them we were like family, so my nickname now is Black MacMagnus. Not sure how I feel about that."

Magnus held his ribs and groaned as he laughed. "Ah, ye are my son now."

After his laughter subsided. Magnus's voice turned serious. "What made ye decide tae come?"

Quentin's voice lowered. "Katie was covered in blood. She was freaking out. It was—"

They both looked over at me. I kept my head down so they couldn't see I was crying.

Magnus said, "Thank ye for your attention on the matter. I am indebted tae ye."

Quentin said, "Don't mention it. I've been working for you for over two years and finally feel like I'm doing something worth the paycheck. Speaking of it, is there something I should be guarding for?"

"Everything, Master Quentin: storms, men with murderous intent, an uncle with a grudge. Twill be verra dangerous in time, but it will take them a bit tae figure out how tae work the vessels and Lady Mairead will be a force for them tae contend with. We have a few days for me tae recover. For now I will need ye tae watch the walls."

Magnus opened a protein bar wrapper and chewed for a moment. "How long has it been since I left?"

"A year, you've been gone a whole year."

"Och, has been long..." his voice trailed off. "Would you give me and Kaitlyn a moment tae speak alone?"

"Yeah, I'll leave this here." There was a small pile of food packages on top of the cooler. He zipped the top closed and left the room to go stand in the hall.

Magnus said, "Kaitlyn, would ye come tae the bed?"

"I don't really want to. I kind of need to be alone over here."

He said, "Och," and sat quietly for a moment then he softly asked, "I was gone for a whole year?"

"Yes."

He slowly stood with a groan and walked to join me by the hearth. He sat in the armchair beside my settee. "I ken ye want tae be alone, but I think there has been too much of that already."

I was sniveling with my tear-stained face and puffy red eyes. "You don't have to take pity on me. I mean, I know I'm really desperately tragic looking, but also, as soon as you're well enough, we'll go, we'll go back to Florida."

He lowered his brow as if trying to understand my words — that familiar look that slammed into me how much I missed him. "Who will go, by 'we,' ye mean all of us?"

"No, I mean me and Quentin. You don't have to come. I meant what I said last night. I'm truly sorry I followed you to the future." I sat up and brushed the hair from my face, trying to not look as weak as I sounded. "I mean, beyond the whole 'I had to murder someone' sorry. I'm also sorry that I interrupted your new life…"

"Kaitlyn, I want tae be verra clear on this conversation, are ye apologizin' for comin' tae the future, for bein' here now?"

"I really believed you were sending me a message. I believed you wanted me. I went to Scotland and dug up the vessel, I thought you would be waiting for me. But instead I—" I gave up trying to be strong and curled up and sobbed into my knees.

"Can ye tell me the story of it?"

"No. I can't tell you. You don't want to know it about me. You don't. It was too awful and if I tell you about it, you'll never be able to get it out of your head. I know I won't be able to stop seeing it — being in that room, knowing there was no one coming. No one wanted to help me. I had to kill him all by myself, because no one wanted to help."

Magnus was quiet.

"And the worst part? He looked just like you."

Magnus scowled and looked down at his hands.

I stared at the hearth.

He had been gone a whole year.

"Tell me something — how long were you gone? What did it feel like to you?"

"I daena ken, weeks. Long enough tae feel the pain of not havin' ye."

"Bullshit, that's not long enough. Not long enough to have another woman, Magnus. Not. Long. Enough."

"Och, finally, tis the story behind your words."

I mocked him in his own voice. "'Aye, Kaitlyn, ye found me out.'" I looked him directly in the eye. "You deserted me and then you had a mistress. I know because he told me about it while he had his filthy hands on me. He told me that you weren't going to rescue me because you had a new woman now."

"Dost ye want tae ken the story of it?"

"What are you going to say? That you left me but you were trying to get home? That the woman didn't mean anything? It does. It means so much that you did that. You left and waited mere weeks and then got another woman to replace me."

Magnus sat quietly.

He started to speak then stopped and started and stopped again. "I winna say she meant nothing. She meant a great many things tae me. She meant I might survive. She meant I had a chance tae kill the king. She meant that if I followed her word I would get tae have a vessel so I could see ye again. I meant it when I said I was coming home tae ye. Always."

"So you were with another woman for me? I wish I didn't know this about you. I wish you would lie and tell me it didn't happen. I wish I never went there and now I wish I never saw you again."

Magnus winced. "Ye daena mean that."

I sniffled. "I don't know what I mean. Beyond that I don't know anything anymore. I'm so fucking angry that this happened to me."

"I wouldna want tae lie tae ye, Kaitlyn. And I daena want tae excuse the wrong that I have done tae ye, but I haena taken another woman in the manner ye speak of — I was a prisoner just as ye were. I wanted tae stay alive." Then he said, "And ye ken why I left, Kaitlyn."

"I did. I used to, but now... It was a whole year and none of it makes sense anymore. You abandoned me." I took a deep breath. "What do you mean, you were really a prisoner?"

"Aye, Donnan kept me locked in my rooms. I was only allowed to leave tae train or tae fight. When I left my rooms I was bound by the wrists. Then she came tae me and offered tae help me. She had a plan tae kill Donnan, but when I agreed tae help she turned it against me and threatened tae tell him..."

He looked at me across the space. "Ye ken the feeling, Kaitlyn, tae have tae do something tae stay alive?"

"Yes, I wanted to stay alive too."

"I am glad of it. Whether ye hate me or love me, I am glad ye kept livin'."

"I am so furious with you."

"You have a right tae be. I winna argue with ye on it."

I huffed at him. "I'm glad you're still alive too."

His voice got really soft. "And even if ye wish ye never saw me again, I am grateful for the chance tae tell ye of it. That I love ye, mo reul-iuil. I haena thought of anything but you."

I looked across the space at him. His face etched with sadness.

I looked away. "I will likely have a scar down my cheek. I haven't looked at it yet. I probably look terrible." A tear slid down my nose.

"I daena see a scar, I see Kaitlyn Campbell. She has battled and won. Tis a story tae your face and a courage I am verra proud of."

"It was really scary."

"Aye. When we were leavin' the castle, I saw the room, Kaitlyn. I can believe that ye were terrified. Twas brutal. And I ken ye say I have much the same face as him but I would beg ye tae look on me without seein' him. I canna alter who he was, but I can be a different sort of man. And I will, I will strive tae be, but twould be terrible if ye canna get past the fact that I am his son. Tae lose ye tae that would be unbearable."

His words were calming me, soothing me. I pulled in a deep breath.

He continued, "I am sorry I dinna send ye the message. That I wasna waitin' for ye when you arrived. That I dinna save ye from the horror of killin' a man. And I ken the despair, I have been inside of it — he made me fight tae the death against men I had nae quarrel with. Tis hard tae forgive myself for. But even when the man has deserved it, twill still take a long time tae forgive yourself."

I rested my cheek on my knees. "I really, really missed you."

"A year is a verra long time. I missed ye too. I ken the length of time I passed was shorter, but daena mean I felt it less."

I nodded.

"I am feelin' a lack of wind again. I may need tae lie down. Quentin also promised some ice cream..."

"I'll dig through the cooler and see if I can find it."

CHAPTER 44

*A*fter assuring us that he could make it to his quarters to sleep after dinner in the Great Hall, Quentin left for the night. I stayed in the room. Magnus and I ate protein bars and jerky, and because there hadn't been enough sleep for days, it was time for bed though it was still light outside.

I helped him get comfortable with the mattress behind him to lean against and the oxygen mask on his face.

Then I sat and stared at my feet.

He asked, "Are ye comin' tae bed?"

"No, I think I'll sit on the settee for a little bit longer."

I woke a few hours later, pretty cold, and it was finally dark. I used my flashlight to look around the room. Magnus had taken the mask off his face but the machine was still whirring. I crept around to turn it off, then adjusted the bear skin so it covered the bare boards on my side of the bed and climbed onto it. I pulled the linen sheet and a woven blanket up over me. I left the flash-light burning to the side for some ambient light.

Just as I settled in, Magnus asked, "Dost ye think about him much?"

"Who?"

"Our bairn. I think on him a lot, how he would have been..."

I blinked back tears in the darkness. "Not really, not anymore. In the beginning I cried about it alot, but I guess I've had longer to deal with it."

"Aye. Still feels verra close tae me."

His hand reached for mine and wrapped around it. Then he pulled, trying to get me to come up, but I resisted. I shook my head rubbing my cheek into the bear fur.

He let go of my hand.

I curled it under my chin. My voice was quiet in the dark-ness. "Were you with her, when I was there?"

"Och Kaitlyn, what good comes of considerin' it?" He exhaled. "We were in a different time. I dinna ken ye were there. I was strugglin' with the idea that ye died centuries before."

"Tell me."

"Aye, Kaitlyn. I winna lie tae ye on it. Aye, I was."

"You left me and I don't know if I can ever trust you again. Did you share a bed with her?"

"Aye. She lived in my rooms. But I was a prisoner, Kaitlyn. I believed ye tae be in the past. I believed I would need tae journey tae ye. I wanted a vessel and I was willin' tae do anythin' tae get to it. Thinking of ye as dead in the past was breakin' me."

I watched the side of his face, the shadows in the semi-darkness.

He exhaled. "I married ye before God. I love ye and I was mourning ye. I was mournin' our son. I beg of ye tae understand and forgive me."

I sat up cross-legged beside him. "I know what it's like to

mourn you, Magnus. But I never invited someone to my bed." I took a deep breath to swallow down the tears. "But I do know it's really hard when someone you love is in the past." I stared at his hand casting long shadows across the sheets. It seemed foreign and I couldn't get used to the fact. "Zach wanted to go with me to Scotland to look for your grave. He thought that would help me deal with my sadness, to know the truth of it."

"Sometimes tae ken the truth is tae make the sadness worse."

"I suppose so." I gingerly put a finger right in the middle of his palm and then slowly let my hand relax and curl up in the middle of his strong hand. I breathed and watched my hand, a perfect fit inside his. It would be good to nestle there but slowly his hand closed around mine and then flashes came — my hand, bloody, tightening, pain, the side of the face as the life drained from it inches from my own, the skin of a strange shoulder as it butted against my mouth, and also in there an imagined image, my husband's hand wrapped around another hand, an unknown hand, securing it.

Not mine.

Mine bloodied. Her's secure.

I pulled my hand from his grip.

"Speak tae me of it, mo reul-iuil."

"I was so happy when I went to Scotland with Quentin and Hayley. I was so excited and hopeful. I was so sure that..."

He reached for my knee but pulled his hand back to the neutral position between us.

"Now I wonder if I'll ever be happy again." I pressed the heels of my hands to my eyes.

"What do you see, Kaitlyn, that is frightenin' ye so much?"

I shook my head.

"I canna sleep. You canna sleep. We may need tae talk of somethin' and twould be best tae say it."

I chewed my lip. "You don't want to know."

"I daena, tae tell the truth, but I have tae."

I closed my eyes. "I see him on me. So close that it's just pieces. His skin. I can smell him. Taste him." I gasped for breath. "And he's dying and struggling and..." I focused on Magnus's hand again. "There's blood, so much blood. And it's on me. And then I see me, alone, underneath. It's hard to describe, like I'm not in my body anymore. And I'm watching my body and it's lost and afraid and begging for someone to help and there are all these faces and then nothingness." I bowed my head. "That's what I see. And when I see you..." I sniffled. "I want to see my husband, but instead I see you on someone else. I don't know what she looks like, but I don't need to. It's just the pieces. Everything is in pieces. I'm in pieces."

"Aye, ye sound verra broken."

I collapsed down to the bed and clutched his hand to my lips. I cried, sobbing against his wedding band. "Why did you do it?"

"You ken why — it goes no deeper, Kaitlyn. There is nae meanin' behind it. Nothing tae tell ye of—"

"Did I do something? Was there something I...?"

"Nae, ye ken the answer tae this, mo ghradh. Twas nae tae do with ye, twas tae survive."

I clutched harder, his fingers wet with my tears. "I don't know if I can bear it."

He breathed out like a sigh. "If ye are nae strong enough, what will happen tae us?"

"I don't know..."

He wriggled his fingers from my grasp and wiped the tears from my cheek. "Then ye need tae be strong enough, mo reuliuil. We are countin' on ye..."

We sat there for so long I forgot he might speak. "Where did ye find the vessel?"

"Where you buried it beside the stone wall."

"When I buried it, I dinna ken why. I dinna ken what I

would need it for, but I buried it there, a place where ye could find it. I dinna dare dream of it but ye did find it. You came, and maybe I wasna waitin' for ye at the front gates, but I did my best when I found ye. I regret I dinna protect ye, but I am grateful ye had the strength tae protect yourself."

His finger stretched along the edge of my lips and traced a line back and forth. Gently.

"And tis a marvel that the stone wall, old in my time was still standin' in yours. Dost ye ken how tae build a stone wall, Kaitlyn?"

I shook my head against the fur of the bedding.

"You take all these rocks, ye place them intae piles accordin' tae size, and then ye begin tae stack them. The rocks are the pieces. The bigger pieces go along the bottom for strength, the smaller pieces go intae the spaces between. Ye ponder it and ye listen tae the pieces. They tell ye where they should go and ye slowly build the wall higher and higher until ye have built a wall with the strength tae last centuries. You may have broken intae pieces, Kaitlyn, but we will take our time. We will talk tae each other about what happened and we will listen tae the story of it. We will laugh with our family and we will cry sometimes when we think about what might have been with our son. Soon we will build ye back tae the strength ye had before."

"The images in my head scare me."

"We will replace them with ones that arna frightenin'."

"Trusting you again scares me."

"I am grateful that ye are brave."

I pressed my cheek to his hand. "Can we go slow?"

He smiled sadly. "Tae build a proper stone wall ye have tae go slow. And tis a good thing, my ribs are too sore tae lift many pieces right now."

While he had been talking about rebuilding my pieces my

hand relaxed and fit within his palm and he closed his hand around mine. And he held it, not tight, but enough.

I thought about the wall and the message he sent me through time — *here is the vessel, I want tae be with ye again.*

"Did we just place the first piece, mo reul-iuil?"

"Yes, we — yes, we placed the first piece." I clicked off the flashlight's beam and tucked it to my chest and slept on the bear skin rug with my hand wrapped within his.

It was all I could do, but it was enough for now.

CHAPTER 45

By mid-morning the next day Magnus felt a lot better, the oxygen treatments, anti-inflammatories, vitamins, and protein were working wonders, and we all decided he could come down to the Great Hall if only for a little while. Quentin went to the hallway so I could help Magnus change because he was still wearing that odd filmy-fabric kilt from the future. Without the underwear though; he took that off hours ago because it, "Was causin' a pain at m'manhood."

First, I gathered the kilt on the belt the way he had shown me so long ago. And he dropped the kilt he was wearing while I averted my eyes because — because I was angry. Because I was so sad. Because it felt like his body wasn't mine to look at anymore.

I helped him pull up the new kilt because though he felt better the pulling and tugging of clothes ached around his middle. It took a bit of time because I wasn't practiced. "Okay, now we get you out of this shirt, which is beginning to reek by the way."

"I will be glad tae have it off, tis too soft. I need the feel of wool and rough linen on my skin." He rubbed the tartan against his thigh. "Tis more familiar."

I smiled. "Keep your good humor, this next part will be difficult." He sat on the bed and I pulled up the bottom of his shirt slowly, gingerly. "Okay, now lift your arms. I'll go quick." He lifted his arms with a grimace and I pulled the shirt up, over, and off, as quickly as I could with as little pain as I could help. I wadded the shirt up and stuffed it in the same bag-pocket where the future-underpants were hidden.

I picked up the new shirt, unfolded it, shook it out to begin to pull over his arms. "I lied, this will be even harder." I turned to him and stopped. I looked. Chest and shoulders and abs and — but — there on his shoulder...

I dropped the shirt and grasped his shoulder and really looked at it. A bitemark. "What the fuck, Magnus. Oh my god." I backed up while he looked down at his shoulder and began to say, "Kaitlyn—" but I was already out the door.

CHAPTER 46

I found Lizbeth in the nursery. "What is it, Kaitlyn?"

"I'm sorry, I keep rushing to you in a state of despair, but—"

She said, "Nae matter in it, tis my family that is causin' it all. If I can help ye, I will do it gladly. Turn around, your bodice is undone."

"Magnus is injured — I have no one to help me dress."

"Magnus usually helps ye? Tis verra handy of him. I will have a woman attend tae ye in the morning from now on, I believe Magnus can stick tae the undressin'."

She laughed until she noticed I wasn't. "Tell me of it, Sister." She tightened the laces across my lower ribs as I pulled my breasts up to the top of the bodice.

"Magnus has taken another woman."

"Oh." She worked on the laces and got them tied. She turned me around, put her hands on my waist, and her head to my forehead for a moment. Then she released me, stepped away, and looked me over. "Twas nae what I expected of him."

"Me neither."

She led me to the hallway. "I am glad of an excuse tae leave, now that I am carryin' a bairn everyone thinks I be necessary in the nursery." She sighed. "I try tae be a terrible mother, yet they keep thinkin' tis my station in life." She chuckled.

Once in the hall she turned to me and held my chin in her hands. "What will ye do about it?"

"I don't know. Everything he says sounds like an excuse. Everything he promises sounds like a lie. I don't know what to do. If I leave him—"

"You canna leave him, Kaitlyn, tis nae possible."

I opened my mouth to argue but remembered the year and closed it.

She said, "You have vowed tae live your life with him and he is a good man, I ken tis true. I have grown up with him. I watched him with Sean and he has always had a loyal heart, and a patient soul. I daena ken what he is about with this, but I daena believe he has it in him tae be the kind of man who would break his vow tae ye."

"I don't think he meant to, it just—"

"Well, it all weighs on ye the same. When a man is lyin' tae ye tis like having a squirmin' pig in your arms. You have tae carry it about with ye all the live-long day when all ye want tae do is drown it in the laundry water."

I winced.

"This is the path ye must walk, Kaitlyn. The path ye chose. You are his wife and he is your husband. Ye have a family now in us, he has a family in yours. You're tied tae each other until death." She smiled sadly.

"What if this is the man he is?"

"What does your heart tell ye?"

"That he means it when he says he'll pick up the pieces, that he loves me."

"Tis much more like the young Magnus I helped tae keep out

of trouble. Och, he and Sean were always in the thick of it. Twas nae easy tae keep them alive some days. Sean has reformed himself by marryin' a God-fearin' woman and doing what she makes him do. But Magnus, I think he was provin' his worth in devotion tae ye. I think he has made a grave mistake in it, and I would believe he is verra afeared about your forgiveness."

"I think so too."

A loud crying sounded from inside the room.

"Sounds much like Jamie," she said and we entered the nursery again. Her son toddled up and she brought him to her lap.

I sat beside her. "When you call Magnus, Young Magnus... Is there an Old Magnus?"

"We have always said it. Old Magnus used tae be around but he haena been here in a long long time. I daena ken if I've seen him since I was a wee bairn. But Young Magnus had the name stick tae him because of it."

A toddler padded by with an unsteady waddle and fell over and stood back up looking adorable and a lot like Baby Ben back home. "Who was Old Magnus related to?"

"I daena ken. He was alone I think."

I smiled at her son and played a round of peekaboo with him. "Enough about me, you have a new husband and you haven't talked of him at all."

"Aye, he was the one I was dreamin' on."

"And by my calculations it took you almost five months to get him to marry you!"

"Five months!" She jokingly exclaimed. "Twas so long!" She laughed merrily. "A few months after the funeral I said tae him, 'I ken what ye need tae have in a wife.' And he said, 'What do I need?' And I said, 'Ye need a young woman who has recently lost her husband and will need a man such as ye tae comfort her.' And he said, 'Och, I should comfort her, should I?' And I said,

'Och aye, ye should comfort her and if ye are willin' ye should let her comfort ye as well,' and he smiled at me, such as this..." she showed how he tilted his head and sized her up, then she said, "and we were married a month later." She grinned.

"That's an awesome story. And are you happy?"

"Verra. Remember how my last husband was nae handsome, or had many wits, or wasna at all kind tae me? My new husband is handsome and kind."

"You didn't mention his wits!"

"He haena got much, but I daena fault him for it. He takes my word on most everythin' so he suits me quite well."

"That does sound perfect."

We quieted and watched the children for a few moments. Then she asked, "How come ye haena had a bairn yet, Kaitlyn?"

"I was pregnant."

"Ye were?"

I nodded. "I lost it."

"That is the history of it then. Young Magnus has lost his way because of it. Tis a hard thing tae lose a bairn. Have ye recovered from it, Sister?"

"A little bit."

"Men are afraid of the mysteries of our bodies, Kaitlyn. They daena ken tae protect us and they feel mighty lost when all their strength and power is for naught. Ye have tae gentle him back tae ye, tell him nae tae be afraid for ye. Show him your strength and comfort each other. Twill be better in time."

"Thank you. That's good advice."

"With my bairn comin' in the winter season plus my husband's, my bairn will number four. I will need tae apply m'self tae bein' capable of it."

"I heard Magnus and Sean talking about your midwife."

"Why were they speakin' on it?"

"It was a while ago, Sean was wonderin' if I might also be a—"

She set her jaw. "Sean Campbell should ken better before he wonders such a thing, I have a half a mind ta—" She took a deep angry breath. "My midwife was accus'd. Twas the physician who started it and a few hateful souls who added tae it. There was nae speakin' on her behalf once the idea had taken root. It began with a word, Kaitlyn, twas all it took. She was a gentle heart and verra wise. I will regret her nae attendin' me this birth."

"Who will be your midwife now?"

"There is one in the village. She will attend me."

"Is she good? I mean, do women make it through...?"

"As ye ken, Kaitlyn, tis a tough journey nae matter the midwife. She is nae my first choice. It is whispered that she daena ken tae be kind. But..." She shook her head. "Twill be fine and I have done so twice already, tis nothin' tae worry on."

"Still I worry."

"I ken, we all do." She squeezed my hand and gave it a nice but not quite comforting pat.

CHAPTER 47

*L*izbeth and I entered the Great Hall looking for the men. It was mostly empty until a large group of boisterous men entered, perhaps thirty men altogether, loud enough to be a hundred. For a moment it was noisy and unsettling and I was furious with him and didn't want to see him but I also kept looking for him in the crowd.

And then there he was.

He came to me — quiet and intent. His eyes had a look to them that reminded me of the day we discussed our wedding across the boardwalk. Not knowing what to say. Not understanding what we each were thinking.

He said, "I was worried ye wouldna be here."

"I'm not the one who leaves." I cut my eyes at him and added, "Where else would I be? There's no where else."

"Och." He shifted. His gaze glanced around the room and then settled back on me.

I asked, "What have you been doing?"

"Quentin and I have been improvin' security. We stationed more men on the walls and have had a strategy meeting with

Uncle Baldie and the Earl. I have explained that there may be trouble followin' us, but I believe the protection is ample."

"That's a relief."

"Aye." We stood awkwardly.

"Kaitlyn..." he shifted. "You haena learned anythin' new. I dinna keep the truth from ye."

"I understand that, but still — seeing it... Once seen, I don't know if I can unsee it."

"I still believe we can build strength from the pieces."

"Yeah... but I tripped on that first piece we placed for our wall."

"Aye, we have tae place another and another." He held a hand out before him, flat. I laid a hand over his. He put a hand on top of mine. "That is how we build."

I nodded.

"Have ye eaten yet? I hear food is about."

He turned to his Uncle Baldie and said, "I am much starved, Uncle, any chance of food appearin' before I fall famish'd tae my grave?"

His Uncle Baldie laughed. "Tis the Earl's schedule we live by here, Young Magnus. Ye needs must be patient. I daena think he has risen yet from his afternoon nap. If we return tae Argyll, then I will ken the food schedule. We will eat on my time." He patted his round stomach. "All the time."

Men sat all around on chairs up and down the table, but also gathered in a seating area to the side and a few smaller tables set up in the corners. Trays of food were placed down the table and then men were serving themselves like a buffet, but messier with way fewer manners. Whisky and beer mugs were passed around and voices were raising with excitement and drink. Magnus took two chairs and turned them around so our back was to the table and we faced the room. Quentin sat beside me. We ate with our plates in our lap.

Sean stood up and said, "Young Magnus, I want tae hear your latest tale. Ye have the pallor of someone who has been defeated on a battlefield though ye are walking around nae yet a ghost."

Magnus smiled. "I haena died yet." He put his plate down on the table behind him and stood to tell his story.

"Since I left here, Brother, I have been tae see the lands of my father."

Uncle Baldie called from his place down the table, "Donnan? I thought he was long dead and I rejoiced tae hear of it."

"Aye, he wasna dead when my story began, and ye were right tae speak of him in that way. I met him and his reputation was much deserved."

Sean boomed, "So tell us the story of it. Ye are talkin' of him as if he has passed."

"Aye, he is nae more, but tis nae his story ye want tae hear, twas my own..." His face turned serious. "While I was in the lands of my father I was made tae fight tae the death in an arena."

One of the men said, "Does this explain your size? You are twice the man ye once were."

"Aye, twas much trainin' tae accomplish it. I became a warrior. I was made tae fight for the throne. I said tae Donnan, 'I daena want your throne,' but he wouldna listen. I had tae meet my Uncle Tanrick in the arena. Have ye met Tanrick, Uncle Baldie?"

"Nae."

"He was verra massive." Magnus spread his arms to show the width of his shoulders. "The fight was nae fair and I told him so. I said, 'Uncle Tanrick, lay down your weapons. I do nae want the throne. I daena want tae fight ye, and without a doubt ye are vanquished where ye stand.'" Magnus's cockiness was met with laughter.

He took a swig of beer while the laughter died down. "But

Tanrick would nae put his weapon down. He wanted tae fight, so I fought him."

"What sword?"

"A broadsword."

"Yet ye stand here and this daena explain the injury tae the ribs, Young Magnus."

"It daena. He fought well, though in the end I defeated him and was declared the victor. People were chantin' my name in the stands." He pulled up the sleeve to show his shoulder, but dropped his sleeve again before he exposed the bite mark. He pointed to the shoulder instead. "I had a deep cut here and here."

"A week later I was called upon tae fight one of Donnan's sons."

"Your own brother?" asked Sean. "Should I be more cautious with ye?"

"I am the same brother ye ken before. As to this brother, I haena ever met him so twas nae difference tae me. I told him I would spare his life if he would place down his axe. I said I dinna want the throne. That I dinna want tae fight, but he never answered. He stared across the battlefield and shifted the axe from hand tae hand. So I fought him. I was declared the winner with three swings. I was verra surprised, I haena fought with an axe before."

Uncle Baldie said. "Whoa ho, young Magnus, ye had two victories then!"

"The chantin' was loud, 'Magnus! Magnus! Magnus!'" He grinned. "I was verra pleased with the victories, but I wasna allowed tae rest for long. Another son of Donnan wanted tae fight me so I was brought to the arena once more."

"What weapon this time?" asked Uncle Baldie.

"This time twas a hammer. Twas blunt and had a heavy head about it. And this brother had been trainin' with the weapon. He had been studyin' my fightin' tae learn how tae defeat me. Tae begin the fight I told him I daena want the throne and tae put down his weapon. He answered, 'I will watch you die at my feet.' Twas his blows that caused m'injuries."

Magnus pretended to swing and then groaned and held his ribs. "He hit me again and again and twas a struggle tae remain standin', but in the end I brought the hammer around and got him tae the ground." He swung toward the ground like he was reliving it. "I killed him after many blows — he dinna die at my feet though, I lay injured on the ground beside him. I was borne away tae the physician after the fight, but I was nae defeated."

Sean said, "Well done brother, tis the Campbell in ye that ye fought so well."

"I was trained by the best."

Uncle Baldie asked, "But what happened tae Donnan?"

Magnus slowed down his bravado and bragging. He was thoughtful for a moment. "Donnan — I daena wish tae waste m'breath on him. Suffice it tae say King Donnan lay dead at the feet of a Campbell."

His audience erupted into laughter and general cheering and across the men Magnus's eyes met mine.

Sean asked, "Tell me, if your father, King Donnan, lies dead in his far-off lands, why are ye here? By my understandin' ye have a throne now. You are a king."

Magnus chuckled. "Were ye nae listenin' tae the story, Sean? I daena want the throne!"

There was a great deal of laughter in the room.

Sean shook his head. "You are willin' tae give up a kingdom, Brother, what for?"

"For Kaitlyn, tae live with Kaitlyn on an island across a far away ocean. Tis an easy trade for me."

Sean waved him away with a hand. "Och, Little Brother, ye are always of a different mind than me." He patted Magnus on the back, overly hard.

Much alcohol was consumed. Many battle stories were told. Most of the men had accents so thick I couldn't understand a word they said, but the pantomimes and facial expressions helped me enjoy it. The whole evening was immensely entertaining.

Quentin stayed sober but looked like he was enjoying himself. Lizbeth smiled whenever our eyes met, a knowing smile, an I'm-supportive-of-you and you're-doing-great smile.

As we sat there in our chairs, side by side, Magnus's hand was resting on his thigh, close to mine. He slowly, very very slowly turned it over, palm up, and then he left it there, open, inviting, tempting.

A few moments later I shifted my hand, slowly, closer and very casually, almost imperceptibly, I placed my hand gingerly in his.

Without looking I felt his hand fold around mine. I took a long breath in and exhaled a long breath out.

And that too was enough for now.

Magnus needed to return to our room. The day had been long and he needed to rest.

We gathered in a small group to say goodnight. Quentin had been sleeping in a guest room of sorts. It was near ours, a sleeping quarters for the men who were casual guests of the castle. Quentin complained, "The room is so full of farts that it's a surprise we didn't suffocate."

He was lobbying to have better quarters, but Sean clapped him on the back as he overheard our discussion. "Black MacMagnus, those are the better quarters. The other option is the nursery with the wailing bairn, or the Great Hall. It may have a better breeze but nae as much comfort."

Later, headed up the hallways, Quentin complained, "By

comfort he means that sack of straw I slept on? I think there were bugs inside."

Magnus said, "Ye canna sleep with me, Master Quentin. The guard is usually stationed on the outside of the door. We'll discuss tomorrow the plan tae get ye home, but twould be great fun tae have ye the next day, will be Lughnasadh, a once in a lifetime tae go to a festival in the far past."

CHAPTER 48

*I*t was still light out though it was night already.

Magnus said, "Come here, Kaitlyn, I will help ye with your laces."

I stood in front of him and he quietly loosened them down the row, pulled them apart, and then we worked together to get the whole thing off. There was always this moment just after where I felt truly free and unrestricted. It was so great to get it off my body.

We were quiet with each other. Nervous.

"I daena think I need the pile of mattress behind m'back." He began to lift the corner but groaned at the pain of lifting it to shake it. "I am beginnin' tae see the end of it, mo reul-iuil. But I will be greatly relieved tae be well again."

"Soon." I poured ibuprofen into my palm and gave it to him with some water. Then I climbed up on the bed and with some effort and a lot of silliness managed to get the heavy sack of straw spread a bit more fairly. Though I kept a bit at the top of his side because I wasn't convinced he wouldn't need it to sleep comfortably.

There was no way I was helping him out of his shirt and frankly if he tried to take it off I would make him keep it on. He didn't try.

He rolled into the bed with something close to his usual movements.

"Do you want to use the oxygen machine tonight?"

"Nae, I think the regular dusty air is good enough for me tonight." He pulled the covers up to his chest. I went around the bed and climbed under the covers. I curled on my side. He was on his back and I watched the side of his face.

"Hi."

He turned his head to face me. "Hello, mo reul-iuil. Sadly, I canna lay on my side comfortably."

"That's okay."

"Dost ye want tae come lay on my arm?" He raised it a bit for me.

"I don't think so. I can't, not yet." I chewed my lip. "But if I can't... What if — what if I'm a big pain in the ass and I need more time... and I don't... and I make you wait..."

"What are ye askin', Kaitlyn?"

"Would you leave me and go back to her?"

His brow furrowed. His face clouded over. "Nae, Kaitlyn. You ken this."

"I don't. And I can be a huge pain in the ass. What if I'm such a pain that you can't stand me anymore? Would you go back to her?"

He took a deep breath.

"If you are such a pain in the arse that I canna bear tae live with ye anymore? What would that be, Kaitlyn, I canna imagine it?"

"Maybe I can never get over this."

"So in this story, ye never forgive me?"

"Or something. Would you?"

He looked at the ceiling and shook his head slowly. "I wouldna, Kaitlyn. I would keep tryin' tae make it right with ye. I hope twould be sooner than later because we have lost time tae make up for. But if tis 'never' I would have tae die tryin'."

"Okay. That's — okay. Thank you, that helps."

He casually placed his hand to his side, up near his shoulder with the palm up, inches from my face. His fingers were curled. They had a relaxed look to them, not stretching for me, not insistent. Waiting.

"I hadn't heard those stories yet. The ones you told tonight. I know you meant them to be funny, but I could hear it behind the story, how awful it must have been."

"Aye, twas a dark time, but let us talk of better things. Tell me of our friends. How is Mistress Hayley?"

"Hayley, um, where to begin?" Our voices were low, in the air just between us. It wasn't dark, but was dimming, the sky turning off our light for us. "Michael is pressuring her to set a date for their wedding. She thinks it's a ruse to get her pregnant. He's been talking about babies too much for her liking. I think so too. He wants a family. So, she came up with a plan — Zombie Runs."

"What is a Zombie?"

"A zombie is a monster. It's the undead, a ghost, but ripped up and mangled and decayed and it, for some reason, wants to eat brains so it chases humans around."

Magnus's eyes were round. "Tis terrible and these exist in your time?"

"No, they don't exist in any time. They're invented monsters, like a fairytale. But someone came up with the idea to have races where actors in zombie costumes chase the runners."

"So tis a race. A footrace? And while ye are runnin' the monsters are chasin' ye?"

"Yep, crazy, huh?"

"Tis nae crazy, sounds fun."

I raised my head up on my hand, leaned on an elbow. "You would think so. There are other ones too. There are races through mud and there are obstacle courses that have rubber hammers and —"

Magnus groaned and held his ribs over-dramatically. "They all sound good but the hammer."

"Okay, zombies only. No hammers. When our lives calm down, we'll sign up for one and do it together."

"Tis a deal."

"But back to Hayley, she is doing these races with Michael. She's getting really into it and signing up for more and more to distract him from wedding planning. It's quite funny, actually. Plus it's part of her mission to stop drinking as much as she does without actually 'not drinking.' She just signed them up for a race where drinking is part of it."

"You drink alcohol and then fight the zombies?"

"No, no, you don't actually fight the zombies. And no swords. They're just actors. You just run from them."

"Ah, that part would be difficult for me."

"I don't know, you're a pretty gentle soul considering."

There was a pause and my hand drifted up and my fingertips settled in the middle of his waiting palm and then they curled like an egg in the middle. He wrapped like a nest around.

I was secure. Safe. Within.

"Tell me of Master James Cook."

"Do you remember his girlfriend, Lee Ann? The one who flirted with you so much?"

"Nae really."

"Good answer. They went out for a long time but they had a terrible breakup because he slept with someone..." My voice faltered. I dropped my head to the mattress, clamped my eyes shut and pulled his knuckles to the bridge of my nose and held it there, tight, clenched, fearful — *skin, blood, life draining out, a struggle, a mouth on Magnus's shoulder* — until I could breathe again. Until I could let it go.

When I opened my eyes again and let go of my grip on Magnus's hand. He kept it there, close to my face, his pinky finger under my nose. The side of his palm against my lips.

I pulled in some necessary air. "Zach and Emma are doing great. Baby Ben is amazing. He walks now."

"Och, he is just gettin' fun."

"Yep, he toddles around and gets into a ton of trouble. It's very cute."

"I can imagine."

"I didn't see him much at first. I didn't see anyone for a while until Hayley made me. It took a lot of forcing me, but sometimes that's for the best. And let's see, there's a new guy in the group, Tyler, he—"

Magnus's head shot up. "Tyler?"

"Yes, he's a friend of Michael's from school. He hangs out in Fernandina now like every weekend — why did you...?"

He searched my face for a moment and then settled his head back down. "Nothing, I just thought I heard the name before."

"Oh, well Tyler hangs out with the group now all the time. He's infuriating. You'll see. He tells me how to do everything like I'm a big idiot. Though he was the one who told me about the storms in Scotland over the ruins of Castle Talsworth."

"A turning point for us."

"True, I just hope it turned us in a good direction."

"I think so. I think every night we share a bed is a good night, Kaitlyn. We will survive the time we spent away from each other."

"How do you know it?"

"I ken it here." He brushed his finger along my lip. "Because when ye talk tae me of our friends I can hear it in your voice — ye are fillin' with hope. You will guide us forward. I daena ken what will happen next but I verra much want ye speakin' tae me through it."

A tear flowed from my eye, down his fingers to my curled fist.

"I daena want tae ruin the evenin' but all this talkin' has worn me out."

"Do you need the machine?"

"Nae, I think that part is behind me."

CHAPTER 49

*E*veryone was preparing for the festival. The castle was bustling with preparations. The fields were full of men bringing in the harvest. Magnus took a long turn watching at the walls, and I spent that time with Lizbeth but then he came to the nursery later. "Good afternoon Lizbeth, might I take Kaitlyn for a time?"

He was so formal it sort of took my breath away.

I rose and followed him to the hall. "I wanted tae walk tae the stables and see the horses. And I wanted ye tae go with me."

"Of course." He held out a hand and we walked through the halls, side by side, my hand in his. Near the bottom of the steps he paused. "Here."

"What is here?"

"Here is where I tried tae get under your skirts so long ago. Remember that night?"

I smiled at the memory of his fumbling desire. "I do."

We began to walk again across the wide foyer and through the courtyard. The sky was high and blue with tufts of clouds rolling across it. Brisk and cool, but a beautiful day all the same. I tucked my other hand around his elbow and held tight to his arm as we traveled across a wide field.

"We aren't going to the stables?"

"Nae, twas just a ruse tae get ye tae come with me for a walk." Without letting go of my hand he wrapped a strong arm around me and pulled me to his front.

We were very close, almost nose to nose, he looking down at me. I looked up into his eyes. "Hello, mo reul-iuil."

"Hi."

"You needed some warm sun on ye."

His face was just right there, so close. I said, "I did. It feels good."

"Close your eyes."

I closed my eyes. Warm sun on my face, my husband's breath on my cheek. I peeked up and his eyes were closed too. His head bowed over me holding me securely around the back. I closed my eyes again and relaxed onto his arm and breathed deeply. I breathed in the scent of the field grasses in the sun — a smell almost like warm bread. There was also the scent of the woods farther along, pine tree and soil, and Magnus with the scent of the world here — woods and castle and wool. His head lowered and the stubble beard he had been growing for the past four days lightly pressed to my temple.

His breath in my ear.

I pressed closer, up, toward him.

And his voice from deep inside rising up to vibrate to my ear. "I have missed ye."

I breathed that in and held it deep inside wrapping around my lungs, filling the spaces that had been so empty for so long.

My hand reached up to steady his face and to pull his lips closer, but I peeked. The images flashed through my mind — images of terror and pain and gore and — I clamped my eyes tight and pressed my forehead to his cheek. Then I tucked my head against his chest and the spell was broken.

He released my arm and we both stepped away from each other. "I'm sorry," I said, "I'm trying. I really am."

I looked at the ground, the woods, the far castle, anywhere but at him. His brow furrowed.

"What is happening tae us, Kaitlyn?"

"I don't know, I just..."

He watched my face. "You just...?"

"I need more time to trust you."

"Aye."

I was so pissed at myself.

He shook his head. "Ye haena forgiven me yet."

"I have. I mean, I understand and I..." My voice trailed off.

He looked away at the horizon and then back at me. "I am sorry, Kaitlyn. I am sorry that I canna tell ye in the right way so that ye ken what I mean. I love ye. I dinna mean tae break ye. I wanted tae save your life."

I watched his face as he spoke. There was pain there. Sadness and despair. It wasn't the face of a liar. I had seen enough of those.

I wrapped my arms around his injured chest, mindful of his hurt ribs, and tucked my head there. I nodded. And I gingerly held on.

I felt his strength. His arms wrapped around my back. His cheek pressed the top of my head.

The more I held him the more I felt loved. Until finally, my voice muffled against his chest, I said, "I know. I understand. I do."

"Ye have forgiven me then?"

I nodded, rubbing my tears into the linen of his shirt. "Yes, I do, I forgive you, but I don't know how to get back there from here. I'm scared that I don't know."

"I daena ken either, mo reul-iuil, I was countin' on ye for the guidance."

He pulled up my chin to meet my lips. I shook my head and pulled away. "We'll figure it out." I pushed the hair from my eyes. "We will, we'll figure it out."

He didn't say anything. He held out his hand and I took it and we walked some more ignoring what had just happened — I couldn't kiss my husband.

I didn't want to.

And I was really really worried about that.

The long hours holding hands with him, watching him do the work of gentling me back to him. It was filling my heart with love. Because Lizbeth had been wrong about that — it wasn't me that needed to do the gentling. It was Magnus.

And he was doing it.

But though I had forgiven him in my heart, I couldn't stop my mind.

My mind kept reliving that feeling of being abandoned, and that struggle, that crime, that brutal death by my hands. The blood on them.

And the woman in his arms.

There was not enough soap in the eighteenth century to clean up this mess.

Not enough showers.

Maybe when we went home and I cleaned some more...

CHAPTER 50

*D*inner was spare that evening. Quentin appeared carrying a plate with a small pile of congealed pudding, and said, as he sat down, "I haven't seen one Ferris wheel for this festival, not one. And no Tilt-a-Whirl. As far as I can tell they're baking a lot of bread. Loaves and loaves of bread."

Magnus said, "There will be a lot of bread."

"Well, good, because I'm hungry. I miss Zach's cooking."

"Aye, me too, will be good tae go home." He leaned in to kiss me on my cheek.

I leaned away. *What the hell, Katie?*

His brow furrowed. He said, "Kaitlyn, we need tae—"

Sean approached and interrupted, "I've been meanin' tae speak tae ye, Brother."

"You have a serious look."

"You said ye daena want your throne." He sat down in the chair beside Magnus.

Magnus chuckled, shaking his head. "Ye got that from my story?"

"Aye, I got that. But there's a problem in your words, Young Magnus. You are forgettin' the truth of it — the king who winna take his throne is a dead king. I daena want tae see ye gone so soon."

Magnus put his hand over mine, protectively, but oh my god, the thought of him on the ground, bloody, dead, hit me hard — begging for help, my hands covered in blood, strangers backing away from the sight of me. Tears welled up and I pulled my hand from under his.

Magnus's eyes cut to the side of my face.

Sean asked, "Who is contestin' it?"

"Everyone, but Uncle Samuel is the biggest concern. He has likely already staked a claim on it."

"Aye ye mentioned he was the one ye feared was coming. I tell ye, Brother, it daena sit well tae have ye in hidin' while lesser men take what is yours. Whether ye want it or not." He put a fist beside Magnus's place setting. "I will protect ye. Your family will protect ye, but I urge ye tae reconsider. The only way Samuel will ken ye are nae comin' for your throne is if ye are dead. He will want tae make certain ye are so, daena give him a chance."

"I understand."

"Good."

"But I am still takin' Kaitlyn to the Island." Magnus's face was solemn as he raised his glass and after a moment of shaking his head Sean raised his glass too.

Sean left. Quentin was deep in conversation with a group of men. Magnus asked, "You are being verra quiet, mo reul-iuil."

I took a deep breath. "This is really hard."

He put his hand out for mine.

I looked down at my own, clasped in my lap.

"You said ye have forgiven me?"

I nodded.

"But still ye arna comfortable with me?"

"I don't know if I'm comfortable with anything anymore. I don't know what to do about it." I looked away.

CHAPTER 51

When we walked upstairs for bed, the stairwell was dark, though it was still pretty bright outside, maybe nine at night.

Magnus seemed thoughtful. We passed that spot where he fumbled with my skirt so long ago without any mention of it. I was worried about that fact. Maybe we had passed the point of no return.

We stopped along the way to pee in the garderobe at the end of our floor. He waited outside for me and then I waited outside for him.

And then we went to our bedroom.

He sat on the bed. "Turn around so I may undo your laces."

I stood in front of him, pulled my hair to the side, and he worked at them for a few minutes. "Take off your belt," he said and I unclasped the buckle. I pulled it free and the big skirt dropped in a puff around the bottom hem of my shift. A moment later he had the end of the laces loosened. He helped push the bodice down to the floor and gave me a hand so I could step from it.

"I can't believe it's not freezing. This is new." I climbed across the bed and under the covers on my side. I waited for him to join me expecting a lot of the same of what we had been doing.

Magnus watched me, his brow drawing down. His eyes squinted in thought. "What dost ye take me for Kaitlyn?"

"Oh, um, my husband?"

"There isna a question about it. I am your husband."

"True."

"I am weary of watchin' ye pull away. You daena ken what ye are about. You are keeping' the battle in your heart and in your mind and ye have brought it into the walls of our home with ye. I daena blame ye for it, but ye canna keep it here. The battle is over Kaitlyn, it has been won. Ye can let it go."

He grasped the bottom of his shirt and pulled it up his body and with a grimace pulled it above his head — muscle-bound arms, shoulders, his abs — *holy shit, Kaitlyn* — He dropped his shirt to the side.

"I don't want you to take it off because of the—"

"I daena care what ye think of my shoulder, Kaitlyn. I have a battle scar. Are ye goin' tae hate the sight of me for it?"

He stared at me long. "You said ye have forgiven me for it. Isna that what ye said?"

"Yes..."

He stood in front of me big and powerful and really incredibly hot. "You have a battle scar and I daena blame ye for it."

"It's different."

"Tis nae different. Twas death or fight. Twas the same for ye?"

I nodded.

"Come stand before me."

"No."

"Aye, ye will Kaitlyn. You ought tae listen tae me and do as I say."

"I don't 'ought' to do anything. I'll leave. I'll run out of here."

"You winna. Because ye are tied tae me and ye daena have anywhere tae go."

I huffed, threw the covers off, and crawled across the bed. With as much drama as I could emote I swung my legs down in front of him but continued to sit.

"Are ye afraid of me, Kaitlyn?" He towered over me. His voice was stern. I had every reason to be afraid of him, but —

"No, I'm not."

His chest rose and fell with his breath. "Why nae? Since I have seen ye last I have killed three men. I did it with decision and satisfaction. The first man I killed with a cut. The last man I bludgeoned. And ye arna afraid of me, Kaitlyn?"

I shook my head.

"Why nae?"

"Because I know you love me, and you would never hurt me."

"And why would I kill those men?"

"Because you had to. Or you would die. And I'm glad you didn't die."

"Aye. But still ye are pullin' away from me."

"I don't really understand why. I just need some more time."

"You daena." He unbuckled his belt. "By my accounts it has been a long year for ye without me. You daena need more time." He dropped the belt to the side. "Did ye choose tae bed another man, Kaitlyn?"

"No."

His kilt dropped to the ground. "So I think it has been time long enough. Ye are probably parched."

I took a deep breath to steady myself. "I had toys."

"I ken these toys ye speak of, I believe ye still missed me."

"I did, I really did, I just need—"

"I winna have ye argue with me on this Kaitlyn. We have wasted too much of our time already. Stand before me."

I looked down at my hands. "It's just that I — I'm dealing with a lot, my hands, I killed him — and —"

"Stand before me Kaitlyn. I winna ask again."

"Jesus Christ, Magnus, you're being kind of a dick." I stood up in front of him.

He was naked. I was clothed, a shift that went from my shoulders to my ankles, a big giant muumuu. His cock stretched between us and I was trying to ignore the fact though also quite amazed by it, actually. By him. And kind of overwhelmed by his power and also super hot for his power. Really. Totally.

He stared down at me. I stared up. "Should I be afraid of ye, Kaitlyn?"

"I don't know." I didn't meet his eyes.

"By my accounts ye could kill me in two ways. Ye could do it in the traditional way. Ye could draw a blade on me and send me tae God. Or ye could look me in the eye and tell me ye daena love me anymore, ye could keep pullin' away. Are ye plannin' tae kill me, Kaitlyn?"

"I'm not planning it, no, I just—"

Very slowly he lowered himself to the ground. He groaned, and with what looked like a lot of pain knelt on one knee.

"What are you doing, Magnus?"

He bowed his head forward and rested it on my hip bone. "You could kill me. You have it within your power tae. Should I be afraid of ye, Kaitlyn?"

"I don't know what to say."

His forehead was against the fabric of my shift, reminding me of the hospital bed, a year ago. *Ye ken I have tae go?*

Tears welled up in my eyes. Without knowing what I was saying I begged, "Don't go, please don't go. I need you."

His voice came from the fabric of my shift. "I ken ye need me. I need ye too. And I winna go anywhere not anymore. Stop pulling away from me."

"I'm scared."

"Ye daena have tae be afraid of me, we already established this." He put his hands on my hips and began bunching the linen up in his fists. I tried to keep it down, but not really trying, just kind of overwhelmed by the fact that it was coming up. He pulled it slowly and methodically until the front of it was bunched to my waist. He pressed his forehead to the pleats of the fabric holding it high, looking down at the naked bottom half of me.

"Put your hands on my shoulders."

I did.

I looked down through my tears at the wide strong back bowed before me. I rubbed my palms along the curve and wrapped them around edge of his shoulders and down the front where they curved to the ground.

I faltered at the spot, now fading, but once a bruise — teeth had touched here.

"I wish it was dark, it would be easier."

He adjusted so he was on both knees, his hands wrapped around me and he spoke into the skin of my stomach. His lips wet, his breath warm. "We arna used tae easy. Tis impossible tae expect it." His hands ran along my hips and cupped my buttocks and pulled me closer. His lips pressed to me. He ran his hands down the back of my thighs and back up and around my ass again and I was beginning to lose my will to resist.

A hand trailed around my hip and found its way between my legs and fingers searched and stroked up and then in. "You are verra wet, mo reul-iuil, ye want me—" I was unable to keep track of what he was actually saying. My hands clasped the back of his head and pulled him closer, oh closer, while his fingers dove and played.

"Take off your shift, Kaitlyn."

"I don't—"

He looked up at me with a sweaty brow, glazed eyes, that out-of-your-head look of desire. "I winna argue with ye about this, take it off. I canna raise my arms high enough tae struggle with ye over it."

I pulled the shift up and over and off.

"Lie down and spread your legs."

"What—?"

He stood with a grimace and planted himself in front of me. So close, his face looking down on mine, breathing, wanting, chest heaving. "Daena argue with me. I am your husband and I am returned from battle and ye should spread your legs and welcome me home."

"Are you serious with—"

"I am verra serious."

"You're scaring me."

"I am nae, ye arna scared of me. Ye should trust me in this."

The look on his face was primal, dark, and wanting, and god I wanted him so bad that all of everything else disappeared.

I lay back on the bed with my thighs clamped together. "But what if I've been in battle too?"

"Aye, mo reul-iuil, ye have, and ye are still fightin'. Ye have lost your way because of it." He put a hand on each of my thighs. "Ye need tae guide us, but ye arna capable of it. I see it in your eyes. Your battle has been too brutal, but ye love me, and ye forgive me, deana ye?"

"Yes." I allowed my thighs to relax.

"So ye should spread your legs for me." He pushed my knees apart, slowly.

"And from this day forward when ye come home ye should say, 'Master Magnus, I am fresh from battle, get ye ontae your back and rise with vigor tae welcome me home." He lowered between my legs.

"Oh, that's what I should say?"

"Aye. I would rise for ye if ye would only ask, but ye haena asked," he kissed up my thigh and licked and nibbled between my legs. "I canna wait anymore."

"God, Magnus."

He licked while his fingers were inside me and then he began to trail his lips up my stomach.

"Wait — don't..."

He paused, his chin pressing on my hipbone. "Daena pull away."

"That's not—" I panted, while trying to speak. "That felt good. I want more."

"Och," his brow raised. "She wants more — what does Madame Campbell need tae say?"

"Master Magnus..." I arched up. "Something about rise — spread my legs—" His fingers shifted inside me.

Ogodogodogod...

"—welcome home... yes."

Through my foggy, out-of-my-mind-ed-ness, I saw him grin up at me. "Och, tis good enough."

He returned to me, arms wrapped around my thighs, hands on my ass, his mouth nestled between my legs. He licked and played there, my moans rising and rising and rising and after long minutes — *ogodogodogodogod* — I burst apart into a million tiny far-flung pieces —

I pulled on his shoulders — *up* — and managed to somehow say — *come* — and he climbed me. He scooped me up and spread me wide and entered me slowly.

And held me and filled me and settled me.

And with his mouth up against my neck, the vibration of his breath against my pulse — *I love ye, mo reul-iuil* — a deep breath and another breath — *I know it, I do. I love you too* — he pulled against me and pushed with me, the beat of us cautious, steady, and slow. Our skin pressed, our bodies clasped. Magnus glistened and I rubbed my forehead on his shoulder and then I kissed the skin there and tasted the salt of him. Magnus. Our movements were small and concentrated. My legs around his back pulling him closer holding him deep within.

The beat of us quickened. I arched back and moaned it to his ear — ogodogod — desperate, intense, driven and I was bursting still, again, and more, until with a groan he finished too and his body grew soft and relaxed within me.

Filling me, wrapping around me. His weight collapsed down. His gravity held me securely to the lumpy mattress on the hard planks of the bed.

He groaned.

"Does it hurt?"

"I'm—" He adjusted his body to the length of me and rested his head on my breast. He swallowed a deep breath and a moment later said, "I needed a better position is all." One of his arms was across me, holding behind my back, arching me toward him.

My arms wrapped around his head, cradling him, his forehead close to my lips. I kissed his hairline. I cradled his jaw in my palm and raised his chin and kissed the bridge of his nose. And then I kissed his eyelid and shimmied down a bit to reach his lips and I kissed him. Our kiss — tender and gentle, welcoming — and as the light was fading from the room, my hands — light, loose, and relaxed floated down to settle softly on him.

"That was..." I didn't know how to finish it — awesome, perfect, necessary all came to mind. I trailed my fingertips down his neck across his shoulder along his bicep to entwine with his waiting hand.

CHAPTER 52

*A*t dawn he whispered. "Good morn, mo reul-iuil."
He had shifted in the night onto his back in a more comfortable position. I was beside him, my hand resting on the front of his shoulder. My lips touched the curve of his tricep. My fingertips brushed his neck. It was all in focus now. His skin. His smell. His taste.

"I love you."

"Say it once more."

"Are you going to be bossy with me again today? I thought you were going to let me go slow."

"Twas slow. Three days is plenty slow enough." He chuckled. "And I am nae commandin', I am askin'. Say it again."

"I love you, Magnus."

"And ye are my wife?"

"I am. I am your wife. And I'm really glad you're back in my arms."

"Aye, tis good."

"And I'm really, really happy you're back between my legs. You rocked my world."

He raised his brow and a cocky smile spread on his face. "Ah, a compliment to my manliness. Ye are a verra good wife." His fingers trailed up and down my arm.

"How long do we have before they come for you again? Before you'll have to go again?"

He raised his head to look me in the eyes. "I am nae goin' anywhere, mo reul-iuil. It has been enough."

"But you have vows, and duties, Lady Mairead, a kingdom..."

"Nae. I have done enough."

I raised up on my forearms to look down at him. "Sean may be right about it though. You can't just turn your back on it."

"Aye..." he sat thoughtful. "I — you are right, I canna. I ken I have a duty tae fulfill. But I vowed tae ye before God that I would tie my life tae yours. How do I reconcile the two?"

I pressed my lips to his shoulder. "I don't know. I only know that I can't let you go again."

"Nor I, mo reul-iuil. You are all that matters tae me — wakin' up beside ye. Tae have ye smile up at me. There is nothing else, but—"

"Magnus, love, don't put a 'but' on that. There is nothing else."

I wrapped around his arm. "I don't know how you reconcile a duty to a violent future-kingdom with your vow to love me in Florida. I don't have an answer. But maybe we don't need an answer today. Maybe all we need is this — waking up beside each other, talking through our day, planning together. This is what we want. So every morning we'll do this."

I clasped his hand in mine. "And if you wake up and look over and I'm not here beside you then we've screwed up somehow and we need to fix that. Together."

I pulled my head up to look down at him with a smile. "Get it? I'm not there, but we still need to fix it 'together'? What I'm saying is 'together.' That's the point."

He chuckled. "From this day forward I will look down for your mornin' smile and if ye are nae sprawled across m'chest I will say, 'Kaitlyn where are ye?' And then we will find ye, together."

"It's a perfect plan."

"I had many dreams of ye, Kaitlyn. They felt so real. I was callin' tae ye and ye couldna hear me."

I rested my chin on his shoulder. "I had dreams like that too. You were with me but I couldn't reach you. Grandma said it's because we are entangled. That when we made the baby I took bits of your DNA and bits of the baby's DNA and I have them inside of me now." A tear slid down my nose. "And so even when you're gone..."

"I winna be gone anymore."

"And even though the baby is gone..."

"He is still a part of ye, mo reul-iuil. He is still with us."

I nodded and sobbed into his chest and he held me while I cried.

Then I said, "I need a Kleenex in the eighteenth century." I laughed through my tears.

"Aye, ye have a bit of it comin' from your nose." I scrambled off the bed for a napkin that Zach packed in the cooler and blew my nose.

I sat on the edge of the bed, naked, fiddling with the now soggy napkin. "I feel a lot better. Not perfect, but having a plan that we'll stay together helps."

"Twill take a long time, mo reul-iuil, tae feel perfect again."

"So tell me about Lunessa Llama's day today." I giggled. "What is it?"

"Lughnasadh is a harvest festival. We will go tae church. There will be much prayin' and blessin' over loaves of bread."

I raised my eyebrows. "Oooh, fun."

He grinned. "Then we will eat bread and we will declare it delicious."

I jokingly grimaced. "There is not enough yoga mat in it."

"Explain what ye just said." His strong hand stroked up and down on my thigh.

"A few years ago it was in the news that there was an ingredient in store-bought bread that was the same ingredient in yoga mats. You know, like that one I keep rolled in the corner of the bedroom?"

"Whatever for?"

"I think it was to make it softer and lighter."

He shrugged, "Well, tis delicious."

"I agree. We should begin to dress though, probably." I stood up, his eyes following me. "This isn't me pulling away."

"I ken."

"Good. Because though that was really hot last night, you probably shouldn't get in the habit of bossing me around like that."

"Only if ye arna listenin' tae me." I rolled my eyes and smacked him playfully on the shoulder.

I pulled the shift over my head covering me completely.

He sighed dramatically. "And the fun is over."

CHAPTER 53

*E*veryone convened in the courtyard. There were people in all states of dress. The Earl and his immediate circle were dressed up. The servants of the castle wore simple clothes. My green and brown tartan dress was the same one I borrowed three days before. Lizbeth was wearing a lovely tartan dress in deep blue. Everyone looked fresh and scrubbed. Many of the women carried baskets with round loaves of bread nestled in linen.

En masse we walked the main path toward the high white steeple of the parish church. Inside, the church was laid out like a square, the pews were dark wood, but the walls were white with a sweeping ceiling above. There was a beautiful stained glass at one end. Magnus led me to a pew near the front and we sat and sat and sat. I used Lizbeth as my model and kept my hands in my lap and my head bowed. The service was very long and very very boring and oh so long. Until finally the baskets were carried by a procession to the front and were blessed one by one.

I whispered to Magnus, "Is that it, we're done?"

"Nae, there will be a wedding too."

"Oh."

A young couple walked toward the front of the chapel and a service began that was familiar from my own wedding, but also foreign, older, ancient-sounding. All our heads were bowed, we were quiet all around. The monotone voice of the minister sounded through the air.

My mind began to wander but then Magnus's hand shifted against my skirts. I looked up to see the couple's hands were bound together. Magnus smiled and gave me a little nod. Then he put his wrist just beside mine. Pressed. After that I listened to the prayer and let the words flow through me, handfasting us again. Magnus and I, bound.

Soon enough we were ushered back outdoors. The sun was heading high, warm on my skin. Families were milling around, talking, and children were playing.

Lizbeth came to me with a basket of flowers. "Flowers tae adorn ye, Kaitlyn." She put two in the front of my bodice and one in the back of my pinned up hair. "Beautiful!" She declared it but I noticed she glanced sadly at the cut on my cheek.

I asked Magnus, "So this is it? Now we feast?"

"Aye. Now we—"

His eyes drew up to the sky.

I followed them.

Across the path and fields, beyond the castle, past the stables and then above the woods — a giant storm, perhaps the biggest storm I'd ever seen: spreading for miles, building, roiling, rolling, climbing. The storm was black as night against the blue sky over-head. Under the cloud bank, in five separate places, funneling, sweeping, tornados touched down. A line of twisting winds across the trees under the clouds like an impenetrable wall. Light-ening arced down from point after point after point. Trees were snapping and falling, fire and smoke rose from the woods.

"Holy shit, Magnus."

"Aye, Kaitlyn. Lizbeth? Get the children, go tae the castle." Magnus turned to the assembled crowds, "Take your families, get to the castle!"

I picked up Lizbeth's son, Jamie, while she grabbed her daughter, and we began to run. Magnus was just behind us yelling directions to Sean and Lizbeth's husband, Liam, as they raced toward the castle. No one really understood why Magnus was commanding them inside but the threat of the storm was enough. They were driven into the castle in fear.

Magnus said, "Take the children to the nursery, I will get Quentin from the walls—"

"No, I don't want to lose you, please." I passed Jamie to the next available arms running by. "Please Magnus."

"Lizbeth, ye get all the women and children tae the nursery." Sean and Liam ran up the steps to the top of the walls. "Follow me close, Kaitlyn."

We raced up the spiraling stone stairs through the east tower to the top of the highest walls. Quentin was already there with Sean, Liam, and more men.

Magnus directed everyone to watch the woods. The storm was dissipating. Smoke billowed from the farthest area, burning trees.

I had my back pressed to the wall, facing the opposite direction, Magnus between me and the view of the woods. I didn't need to see, I just needed to be near Magnus.

Magnus and Quentin were in a quiet discussion. They were checking Quentin's pistols and the gun Magnus brought with him from the future.

"Are we escaping?" I asked.

Quentin and Magnus continued to confer.

I asked, "Are they coming, what's our plan?"

More discussion and then Magnus finally included me. "We believe we will be safe here, Kaitlyn, tis a castle, fortified, and we have arms. When I was there, I saw on the news a great many terrible weapons, but we daena ken what they have brought."

"Okay. Okay, so we'll just hunker down. That makes sense." I said, like saying it actually made it so.

And then there was a buzzing noise, loud, like engines, motorized, coming through the silence of the ancient forest. A forest in the eighteenth century, a forest that wasn't supposed to have engines inside of it. And from the edge of the woods, flying up from the trees, five drones.

Their noise was loud. Sean and Liam clapped their hands to their ears. The drones sped toward us, low across the fields. Magnus asked, "What are they Master Quentin?"

"Drones, a kind of weapon, we need to get off the—"

The drones swept up the castle walls in unison and then leveled at the top.

And that's when they began shooting.

Magnus grabbed my hand and pulled me fast to the stairwell of the castle tower. Men were diving and scrambling into the stairwells for cover. Quentin was yelling, "Off the walls, off the walls!"

The gunfire was all around us. The stone of the castle was cracking and chunks of rock crumbled to the ground.

Quentin ducked behind the parapet wall and shot at the drones with his pistols.

The tower stairs were packed with men: yelling, panicked, confused.

The buzzing sound traveled away down the castle walls and then more shooting sounded below — glass shattering. The nice windows, the ones the Earl was incredibly proud of, were being destroyed by the drones. Quentin met us in the stairwell. "I shot one down, but at least one entered the castle. And they aren't flying on their own."

"What dost ye mean?"

"There are men in the woods."

Magnus asked Sean, "How many guns do we have?"

Sean asked, "Are they birds?"

"I haena time tae explain. They are weapons. We need men tae go down and protect the women and children."

Sean gave a command and men above us and below us on the stairs descended with their flintlock pistols drawn.

I asked, "You have the vessels?"

"Aye, both are in my sporran. But we have tae protect—"

From outside the stairwell the buzzing of the drones amplified. So loud it confused my senses. Quentin, Sean, Liam, Magnus and I raced to the edge of the wall.

Coming from the trees raced five vehicles. Much like all-terrain vehicles, they were each driven by one man. The two drones circled them overhead. The vehicles split into two groups. Three raced around the castle one direction. Two raced around the castle in the other and they roared and sped around for long minutes.

The circling terrified me.

The drones swerved and dipped overhead. One drone split from the vehicles and climbed the wall towards us shooting at the stone of the castle. Magnus stood and shot multiple times until the drone fell crashing to the field below.

Quentin yelled over the insane level of noise outside. "Anyone without a gun can throw rocks at the drones, anything heavy. Knock it from the sky."

Sean began passing those instructions to the men around them.

Quentin said, "There's only one drone left out there, the other two are inside the castle. I'll go in!"

Magnus said, "When ye finish it, meet me at the doors tae the Great Hall."

Quentin ran down the steps.

Sean, Liam, Magnus and I watched the action below. The vehicles were circling, revving engines, roaring and terrifying. Magnus shot at the drone and it dove closer. He ducked behind the wall.

Sean stuck his head up and looked over. "Young Magnus, what are they doin' now?"

One of the vehicles was stopped. "I daena ken."

Magnus crouched and raced to a position with a better view. I crouched and followed. Magnus looked over the wall. "What are they doin', Kaitlyn?"

I leaned over to see, trying to make sense of it. The man was attaching a bundle of something to the gate at the front of the—

"It's a bomb, Magnus, we need everyone away from the front of the castle now. Off these walls."

Magnus began urgently waving his arms to get the attention of the other men up and down the parapet. "Get off the walls!" He yelled over the racket of the insane machines below, "Get away from the front gate!"

We crouched and ran along the wall to the far opposite corner when the drone emerged again to shoot from above. Magnus ducked, pulled me to a stop, and stood and shot at the drone until it fell and crashed against the bricks below. "Run, run, run," he yelled.

We escaped into the tower stairwell, and fled down toward the ground floor below. I was tripping and sliding behind Magnus.

As we emerged from the stairwell a deafening explosion knocked me back against the bricks. My ears were ringing. Magnus threw his arms across me protectively. "Are ye okay, Kaitlyn?"

I clutched his shoulder. "I think so."

Then the vehicle that set the bomb drove over the rubble

through the dust and mayhem and right into the middle of the castle. Magnus shoved me into an alcove. "Stay here!"

He rushed toward the edges of the courtyard where the other men were stationed. I covered my ears and watched as a drone dipped and flew around inside the courtyard shooting indiscriminately.

Magnus from one side, Sean from another, Liam in a far corner, and more men fired and threw rocks until finally the first vehicle driver was slumped over in his seat. But a second vehicle drove over the ruins of the gate, entered the courtyard, and began spinning wildly, its machine guns shooting at anything that moved or didn't. Hunks of brick crumbled from the walls. A wooden eave fell to the ground in splinters.

I escaped into the stairwell and a moment later Magnus was behind me. "Go up, go up!" At the top of the stairs Magnus yelled, "Go tae the Great Hall, Kaitlyn, get Master Quentin, tell him we need him in the courtyard." He flung the door open and I raced.

I was running with all my might terrified — what were we going to do? Quentin rushed to meet me. I was panting and could barely speak. "Magnus, he needs — down—" I pointed at the stairwell. "Courtyard."

Quentin said, "You stay here."

"No. Not. I'm with Magnus." I followed him stumbling down the steps. "Careful—" I warned as he stuck his head around the wall to scope the action.

"Shit, that's some fucked up shit, Katie." The noise was deafening — shooting, yelling, the engines, bricks crashing. Quentin held a pistol. "We are seriously outgunned." He looked back around the wall for a second. "Of course this is cool as fuck. A science fiction battle in a medieval castle. Awesome."

Magnus raced over to us from across the courtyard. "There is a weapon ye could use, Master Quentin — would ye ken how tae?" The courtyard was full of rubble. A vehicle was spinning and shooting but another one sat idle in the middle of the havoc.

"I can figure it out."

The noise was so loud I was sure it was destroying my eardrums.

Magnus yelled, "Ye will have tae figure it quickly, three more ridin' machines are outside. They are circlin' and will come inside in a moment. Can ye get tae the weapon?"

Quentin looked around the wall and pulled back. "I can get to it while the other is turned away."

Sean raced into the stairwell with us. "What is happening, Magnus?"

"Tis a war from my kingdom, Sean. I canna explain more. Quentin says he can ride one of the weapons. Twill help tae have a—"

I clutched his arm. "We have to go, Magnus. They're after you."

"I canna leave my family—"

Quentin said, "You can, you have to. They're following the vessels. It's what you said, they track the vessels."

I said, "You know you can't stay. We have to go."

Magnus looked uncertain. "The walls have been breached — more men might be comin'."

Quentin said, "Yeah, and they're going to take apart this castle until they have you. You have to hide better than this. It's unsafe to have you here."

Sean was looking from face to face. "If this is true, Brother, ye have tae take the battle from our walls. The weapons are takin' a deadly toll, we have lost two men already."

"We have to go, Magnus."

The machine gun sprayed bullets across the wall near us. It was loud and terrifying. My skin crawled. I clutched Magnus's arm and kept my head ducked. "The other vehicles are coming. We have to hurry."

Magnus nodded. "Quentin, ye have a plan tae get us away?"

"I have a plan to get you and Katie away. Katie, you think you can drive one of those vehicles?"

"What? Yes, maybe. I drove an ATV once. I mean probably. Where will you be?"

"I'm going to help protect the castle. I'm the only one with modern tactical experience. So I'll stay. You're going to drive out of the castle to the west while I cover you. Then you'll time jump."

"Okay, we'll leave you one of the vessels—"

"Nope, you'll take all of them. They're tracking them, you'll take them away."

"Quentin!"

He smiled, "Hey, it is what it is. I'm the only one here who knows how to work any of these machines, except you and you need to get to safety. It's what you pay me for." He leaned out from behind the wall to check on the chaos. "Besides, you'll come back and get me when you get the chance. You have to visit your family." He checked his ammunition clip and slammed it back. "When I get to the vehicle, Boss, I'll distract the other guy, you shoot him from here. Then we'll have two." He grinned, his fingers counted down, three, two, one — and he was gone.

I couldn't watch. Magnus looked around the wall and I hid behind his arm. The shooting was crazy and continuous and loud and scary.

Magnus said, "He has it."

And then another gun was firing, doubling the noise.

I closed my eyes as Magnus, from just outside the confines of our stairwell, fired his future pistol and Sean fired a flintlock pistol aiming for the man driving the second vehicle until finally

Quentin's voice, "Boss! Come get on this one. I'll teach you how to shoot it before the next vehicle comes in!"

Magnus said, "Sean, watch over Kaitlyn." He raced away across the courtyard for the newly vacated vehicle. My heart followed him. *Oh god oh god please keep him safe.* Quentin drove his vehicle up beside Magnus's and they discussed the controls for a moment while Magnus pushed buttons on the dashboard.

The love of my life didn't know how to work a microwave and he was going to defend a castle with future tech none of us had ever seen before.

A second later he and Quentin had their weapons aimed at the big gaping hole of the front gate as the next vehicle came through and the next and then the next. I kept my head down between my knees. The battle was loud and long and terrifying. Sean with his flintlock kept reloading and shooting. I took a peek at his face — stoic, focused.

When he ran out of bullets he picked up stones and heavy rocks from the rubble around us, hurling them at the attackers while their backs were turned.

Finally, the shooting subsided and the courtyard fell quiet. Magnus and Quentin rushed from man to man, checking their pockets and clothes and tossing them off the vehicles.

Quentin yelled, "I can't find it. None of these men are carrying it."

Magnus said, "There's someone else then."

Quentin said, "The men controlling the drones are out there too."

The two ran to the front gate and stood scanning the woods.

Then Magnus rushed to my side, "Kaitlyn, we must away. Whoever carried the vessel isn't here in the castle — there may be more coming." He said to Sean, "I am terribly sorry tae leave ye when the walls have been breached, but Quentin will stand guard, treat him well."

"Aye, go and if your destination is yet undecided, I recommend takin' the fight tae them. Your kingdom is at stake."

Magnus shook his head. "Maybe ye haena heard, Sean, I daena want the throne."

"I have heard it, and next I see of ye, I will need a full accounting of the magic here."

"You'll have it when I return. Keep Lizbeth and your Maggie and the bairn safe. I will see ye soon. Take care of Master Quentin, he is a good man."

Magnus grasped my hand. "Ready Kaitlyn?"

"Ready."

We left the safety of the stairwell to race across the ruined courtyard, full of stone rubble, debris, and smoke, to one of the vehicles. I climbed onto the seat.

Quentin drove his vehicle forward with jerks beside me. "It's straightforward. Gas here, brake here." I revved it. Magnus climbed on behind me. Quentin said, "Hold on tight, Boss, Katie is wild on a motorcycle."

"That was a dirt bike, ten years ago." I sped forward and just about crashed us into a pile of stone. "No worries I got this!"

Quentin pulled up beside me again. "See this button? It makes it go bang bang bang at the bad guys."

"Awesome, but hopefully they're all dead. I'll leave this at the trees to the west. And you might want to clean up this mess. All this tech is going to freak out the Campbells."

"I'll figure something out. But in the meantime I'll teach a Campbell or two to use them to protect the walls in case there's a bad guy lurking in the woods. Or more coming because they don't know you're gone. Or whatever the fuck these assholes are up to. I'll see you guys in a couple of centuries. Oh and Boss, can I take your room?"

Magnus said, "We will see ye soon, thank you for your

protection." He passed him his gun. Over his shoulder he yelled, "Sean, give Master Quentin my room."

I revved the machine and we shot forward over piles of rubble toward what used to be the main gate. This castle wouldn't hold against more attacks. Even with Quentin protecting the walls. We had to leave to draw them away.

Magnus's arms around me, I drove the vehicle around the back of the castle. Then I sped us across the fields bouncing over rocks and ditches toward the forest on the west side.

Magnus adjusted in his seat, looking behind us, checking the sky. "No one is comin'."

"Good," but I still drove like a maniac.

"Kaitlyn, ye could go a wee bit slower."

I joked, "This is plenty slow enough!" And pulled it into a turn, spraying up dirt, skidding to a stop near the trees. We both hit the ground and ran to the woods.

Magnus had one of the vessels in his hand — "What date, Kaitlyn?"

Magnus twisted the vessel, reciting the numbers, and suddenly I was lifted and slammed and went crashing through pain into another century.

CHAPTER 54

cool wind was blowing across my cheeks. I pulled my eyes open. I was in the sand, face to the sky. I groaned. "Magnus?"

He was sitting beside me, looking out over the ocean, his hand on my hip. Attentive, guarding.

I forced myself to sit up and leaned my head on his shoulder. We needed a moment to catch our breath. The day was a perfect all-one-shade day — a beige, cloud-covered sky, the ocean all white foam and shades of grey, the sand pale as if the color had been drained from it all and we were left in a monochromatic world. I could deal with it better after the stark light and dark of the past and future. This was our present.

As my grandfather used to say, "This day is fair to middling."

Something was scratching me deep in my bodice. I dug between my breasts and pulled out one of the flowers Lizbeth had placed there hours before. A flower, a three hundred-year-old flower. I would need to press it in a book, keep it forever.

I wrapped a hand around his bicep and we sat together breathing in and out watching the surf. A lone gull flew overhead. The seagrass bowed. Magnus's hair waved with the wind. And when I looked up and caught his eye he smiled, a slow smile, a meant for me smile. The crinkle at the edge of his eye was there within reach.

I asked, "How can you be smiling, Magnus? We have so much to do. We have to hide these vessels. Find somewhere new to live. Rescue Zach and Emma from her parents's house. Find a phone. See my grandmother. Oh and walk home. Also I don't know if I'll be able to find a key to my apartment. That doesn't even include coming up with a plan to go rescue Quentin and somehow secure all those weapons. And lastly, we are being chased through time."

He raised his brow. "You forgot tae mention that I am verra hungry."

"That's always at the top of your list."

"Tis all I have on my list, I leave the list making tae ye."

He rubbed a finger along the back of my hand. "And I ken we have a great deal tae do, mo reul-iuil. I am smilin' because I finally made it back home with ye."

CHAPTER 55

My grandma cried when she saw him. They sat together on the edge of her bed, his strong arm around her, her soft fuzz of white hair against his shoulder, and talked about how much she missed Jack. Because Magnus here now, this age, was the same as Magnus then, and the whole thing caused her to conflate the two times — Jack here, Jack gone, Jack young and Magnus. The un-aging Magnus reminded her of those young days with her husband. And I couldn't hear most of it, as it was whispered between them, but it was sweet and intimate and sad.

"...I miss him so much..."

"...I ken, and ye will see him someday, Madame Barb..."

I sat in the corner, unheeded, unnecessary, but that was okay. Because the strong arm of my husband comforting my grand-mother was a balm on my tender spots too.

When we left her room and walked to the lobby and looked out the front windows it was pouring down rain outside. The car was across a windswept, rain-covered parking lot. Magnus said, "Looks like ye will be getting wet. Tis nothing I can do for ye about it."

In answer I folded into his arms. "Thank you. It means so much to me that..."

He kissed the top of my hair. "You daena need tae say it. She is part of our family, Kaitlyn, and I am sorry I was gone for so long."

CHAPTER 56

*H*ayley was the first guest to arrive. "I brought Scotch whisky!" She bustled into the living room and hugged me and kissed me on both cheeks. "It's meant to be ironic!"

I relieved her of the bottle and carried it to our stuffed liquor cabinet. "You didn't have to bring presents. You've been here every day. You helped us move in."

"Plus I found you the place, but still the first party deserves a present." She spun around while taking her jacket off. "You hung pictures. This has a much better vibe than your last place."

I followed her eyes. There was the photo of our dinner after our wedding hanging in the living room. A selfie we took at Disney World placed on the mantle. The photo of Magnus that I took in 1702 was printed and framed and hanging as well. If anyone asked he was on his land in Scotland. The date need not apply.

Beside that? One of the five paintings I owned that looked suspiciously as if it was painted by Pablo Picasso. With a signature that said as much. This was something I needed to handle someday.

Ben was happily banging on the tray of his high chair. Emma was arranging appetizers on a platter. Zach was bustling in the kitchen preparing dinner for twenty. Thankfully this kitchen was four times as big as the apartment's kitchen.

Hayley did well finding the house for us. Signing the lease for me. Money-laundering the payments through her own account. She was doing everything she could to help us hide.

Hayley went to the sliding doors and looked out over the beach. "Too bad it's cold out there today. Your deck is awesome."

"Yep, we maybe should have checked the weather before we planned the housewarming. But that's literally what it's called — a *housewarming*. Not a deck-party. So it's better anyway, more literal."

"I thought all you did was check the weather?" She gestured at the Weather Channel beaming across the room from the tv on the wall.

I said, "Yeah, well as you know, we're especially interested in the weather over Michael's uncle's unused land near Gainesville. So far so good. No storms over the vessels."

"So if there are storms you'll drive down to protect them?"

"Not if, when — *when* there are storms. We have the shovels packed in the trunk of the Mustang for when it happens. Speaking of Michael's uncle, when does Michael get here?"

"A few moments. He's bringing Tyler again."

"Seriously? Well, at least he'll get to meet Magnus, then he can stop being interested in me at all."

"You are so full of yourself, maybe he's here because he likes to spend every weekend with Michael?"

"Right, are you hearing yourself?"

She chuckled. "Though as you mention it he didn't come once while you were gone."

"See?"

"I do see, I also see that my hand has yet to be holding a drink. Zach! I'm practically your sister-in-law and I'm about to die of thirst over here."

Zach said, "When ya gonna go ahead and marry him, anyway? It would be a lot fuckin' easier to take orders from you if you were a relative instead of just some chick at a party." He brought her a glass of wine and kissed her hello on the cheek.

"You see what I'm dealing with here, Katie, literally everyone is pressuring me." She sighed over-dramatically. "I'll have to sign us up for another race. I'm going to run out of the fun ones. I'll be forced to do an Iron Man."

We sat down in the living room. It was decorated beach house modern, but in pale blues and greens instead of the peaches and pinks of our last house.

It suited us better, more wood, a little smaller. Though it had enough room for Zach's family to live here too. There was a lot less glass, plastic, and chrome. Best part? Lady Mairead had never ever been here. She had never even been to the north end of the Island.

She would have a very hard time finding us.

We had no paper trail at all. Magnus's uncle Samuel would never find us.

But that didn't mean they wouldn't try.

And it didn't mean we could ever stop hiding.

As Magnus explained — all it took was dropping our guard once ten years from now and our whole history would be known. I always thought of time as linear, but from the future looking back, each of our individual histories became flattened. My entire life was a long line, but within the longer line of history each life was just a vertical notch down the horizontal string marking the centuries.

Three hundred years from now my entire life would be

summed up in the dash between my birth year and my death year. Kaitlyn Campbell lived from this date until this date. Even if I hid my entire life, well, my obituary might include my address and then I would be found.

There was no hiding from a future. Unless you always hid. So we would.

Michael walked in a moment later, James right behind him, then Tyler too. I welcomed them all. "Where's Magnus?" James asked.

"Getting dressed, we visited my grandmother this morning for the first time and then he had a training session this afternoon. I haven't even seen him yet this evening."

"Cool, I haven't seen him since he got back from Scotland."

Emma brought a tray of appetizers to the table. Another larger crowd appeared, more friends and acquaintances, until we had twenty people easily. We stood around the table and talked and laughed, a full living room, lots of friends. And then a few minutes later from down the hallway came Magnus. Carrying his sword in its sheath. Wearing his kilt, a linen shirt. He was so — awesome. He ran his hand through his damp hair, leaned his sword in the corner, and then his eyes found mine in the crowd.

Aye.

Yes.

He came directly to me and swept me into an arm and kissed me in greeting. Then he was introduced to the guests he didn't know and shook hands and hugged with the guests he did. "Master Cook! Tis good tae see ye."

They did that man hug with the pat on the back. James immediately said, "So explain about Quentin?"

"Och aye, I had a need for him tae remain in Scotland for a time. He's a good man tae handle my business for me."

James grinned. "Well, okay. I mean, he's been my friend since we were six years old but I don't think anyone thinks of him as the kind of guy that can 'handle business'."

"Och." Magnus drew his brow. He looked down at his beer. "Ye are sayin' Quentin is nae capable? I have found him tae be brave and loyal and able tae handle everything I need done. Ye winna hear me sayin' a word about him that is nae filled with gratitude."

James laughed. "Are we talking about the same guy?"

I said, "James, you and Quentin have a long history. You remember him making a lot of mistakes, but as far as Magnus and I are concerned, Quentin is a hero. I won't accept anyone talking shit about him in my house. Even in a 'friendly' way."

James put his hands up. "Okay, okay. I get it. And he served in the military. You're right, he's a hero. Plus he's getting to rewrite history. Wish I could do that sometimes." He raised his eyes to mine.

"Who are you talking about rewriting your history with, me? Lee Ann? Every girl you ever slept with? You don't have to rewrite your past. You have to do everything with your dick differently from this day forward. With new people. Sheesh." I rolled my eyes at Hayley and giggled while we each took a drink.

I glanced over at Magnus. He smiled at me. I smiled back. And the whole night was a lot like that, through tray after tray of appetizers and conversation with all those people. He caught my eye. He lingered on my face. He hung on my words.

Zach and Emma brought out the actual dinner after we were already too full to eat it. Magnus joked that Zach was making up for lost time and shoveled in a big bite.

Michael joked, "We'll have to hire you to cater our wedding, right Hayley?" Her eyes went wide.

Zach said, "Well, about that, baby brother, I'm not really a 'for hire' caterer. I have a fucking job." He placed a tray down on the table.

Michael said, "I know, I just meant—"

"I know what you meant. I'll cater your wedding as a gift because I have a job. I have a family. I have a home. I don't need anyone's charity."

All eyes were on Zach. He ran his hands through his hair with a groan. Then he said, "You know what? I meant this to happen differently..." He looked across the table where Emma sat in front of her plate of food. "Emma, I've been planning to ask you to marry me. I wanted to do it when I drove you home from our first date four years ago, but I came up with a ton of bullshit reasons not to, like marriage isn't cool enough or that I didn't need a contract to prove how I feel." He came around the table and pushed her chair back and kneeled in front of it. "Since then I've wanted to marry you every single day but I've been scared to ask."

Emma had tears rolling down her cheeks. "You were scared to ask?"

"Terrified. What if you said no?"

"We have a baby."

"No one has ever called me smart." He took her hand and held it in her lap. "Every time someone told me I needed to marry you it got worse. I didn't want you to think I was being forced. You deserve so much better than that. You deserve the kind of guy who drops to his knee after the first date."

"I don't know, I thought marriage was pretty uncool for a while there too."

"Yeah, well, I definitely should have dropped to a knee when Ben was born. There's no excuse. I love you. I'm not being forced. I want to marry you. I always have. Will you marry me? And before anyone starts asking, no, I didn't buy a fucking ring, I didn't plan this through, though I — I will buy you a ring. You can pick it out."

Emma said, "Yes."

Tears were rolling down my cheeks. Magnus took my hand.

Zach and Emma spoke to each other, little whispers, "Really?" and "Of course" and "I love you."

Magnus stood and said, "I dinna ken I would get tae see ye become a husband, Master Zach, but I always kent ye would make a fine one." He raised his glass. "A h-uile là sona dhuibh 's gun là idir dona dhuib. May all your days be joyous. Slainte."

We all said, "Slainte!" and everyone drank. And we ate dinner, drank too much, planned a wedding, and laughed.

Then dinner was over and Magnus stood in the living room in front of our big screen tv watching the weather. Zach and I had taught him how to watch it — how to read the radar. How the graphs worked. What the predictions meant. Though he didn't need the predictions, our storms would be a surprise.

Magnus asked Tyler a question about a nor'easter that was predicted for the following week and Tyler stood beside him and they talked about the weather for a while.

Hayley was talking with Michael and then turned to me. "Katie, help me! Michael can't do the Warrior Dash this weekend — can you come? Can you do it with me? Remember you owe me for the whole deserting me in Scotland thing?"

My eyes went to Magnus. "Maybe, if—"

"I'll ask him. Magnus, can Katie run the Warrior Dash with me this weekend? You can come cheer her on."

Magnus came to the dining room table with a big smile. "Kaitlyn, ye would want tae? I wanted tae do one with ye, but my ribs arna good enough."

"I would, it sounds awesome. Okay Hayley, count me in."

He joked, "Would monsters be chasin' her? I would have trouble nae drawin' my sword tae protect her and Quentin isna here tae stop me."

Zach laughed. "I'll come watch. I'll keep you from drawing your sword."

Hayley said, "Besides there are no monsters, this is just an obstacle course."

Zach worked on his phone and brought up the website for the Warrior Dash and showed the main photo to Magnus.

His eyes got big. "Aye, Kaitlyn will race it and win it."

I laughed. "Well, I doubt I'll win it, but it sounds like you're going to make a great cheering section."

Magnus put his hands around his mouth and pretended to chant. "Presenting Madame Kaitlyn Campbell of the Campbells of Balloch on the south bank of the River Tay now living in Fernandina Beach!"

Zach laughed. "Or Katie! Katie! Katie!"

Magnus grinned. "That has a better sound."

Tyler asked, "Are you sure? I mean, Katie hasn't been training, right? Lots of people train for these things, she could get hurt."

Magnus looked at Tyler incredulously. "What are ye sayin', ye daena believe Kaitlyn can do the race?"

Hayley said, "It's just a short one. It's no big deal. If I can do it, she can do it."

Tyler said, "I mean I don't know, I just thought she might want—"

Magnus asked, "Kaitlyn, ye want tae do the race?"

I swigged from my beer wiped my mouth on my arm. "Now more than ever."

Magnus tilted his head back with his cocky grin. "At our home in Scotland Kaitlyn must cross an obstacle course such as this just tae get tae the chamberpot. I think she can crawl through a mud pit if she wants tae, but we will let her worry on the trainin' she needs."

He met my eyes.

And the party just kept getting better from there. Then Magnus walked by my chair and squeezed my hand. He disappeared into the kitchen and came back a moment later. He leaned to my ear. "Chef Zach has said twill be a half hour until dessert is served. I ken it may be complicated but could ye tell the guests ye need tae step from the room for a moment?"

My eyes went big. "For what, is everything okay?"

He whispered, "Tis nae a problem, mo reul-iuil, tis that I want ye."

I giggled, "Um yes, just a minute, let me make it look casual."

I turned to Hayley and we spoke for a second about the new Ariana Grande album. My eyes followed Magnus as he walked around the table talking to James, making a joke with Michael, raising his brow, grinning at me, and gesturing with his head toward our door.

Finally I stood and excused myself for a few minutes and walked down the hallway to our room.

A moment later Magnus entered and locked the door.

He folded me in his arms. "Thank ye. I saw ye across the room and thought, 'I want her. Do I have tae wait for her? Haena there been enough waiting?'" We kissed as his hands traveled up and down my back. "Tis nae fair tae leave our guests, but..."

"They'll understand. You've been gone a long time."

"And we need tae practice in our new bedroom. Tis a new situation for the bed. We need tae learn tae navigate it—"

"Are you saying you needed a booty call because our bed is facing a new direction?"

His lips paused on my neck. "What is a 'booty call?'"

I giggled. "Why do I speak during these things? I should know better."

He pulled my dress over my head. I was wearing his favorite color and — it worked.

His hands ran down my naked back. "Your undergarments, Madame Campbell, are verra wee."

I pulled up the front of his kilt. "Your undergarments, Master Magnus, are non-existent."

He sat on the bed. Then lay back, his calves hanging down, his kilt at his waist, his smile cocky. With his hand he gestured 'climb on,' and oh yes, I climbed on. "Tis so I can get tae the business of ye easier." His hands helped pull me down settled on his lap. I moaned and pressed my palms to his chest.

He winced.

"Sorry, love." I moved my hands to his biceps and held on while we moved against each other. I arched back enjoying the view, my power, him.

Then I folded down over him and pressed my face to his cheek and breathed him in — the scent of toiletries, soaps, clean water, the smell of civilization, but underneath it, his own scent, mingled with mine, a part of me.

Just as I was a part of him.

We had been separated, but found each other again. And in the days since we had entangled even more. Doing the hard work of building me up and rebuilding our marriage. The easy work of loving each other through it.

Like most moments with him, naked and vulnerable, tears welled up in my eyes. Because there had been so much.

Just. So. Much.

But I loved him.

And he loved me.

And that was how we would live on...

The End

THANK YOU

This is still not the true end of Magnus and Kaitlyn. There are more chapters in their story. If you need help getting through the pause before the next book, there is a FB group here: Kaitlyn and the Highlander Group

Thank you for sticking with this tale. I wanted to write about a grand love, a marriage, that lasts for a long long time. I also wanted to write an adventure. And I wanted to make it fun. The world is full of entertainment and I appreciate that you chose to spend even more time with Magnus and Kaitlyn. I just love them and wish them the best life, I will do my best to write it well.

As you know, reviews are the best social proof a book can have, and I would greatly appreciate your review on these books.

Kaitlyn and the Highlander (Book 1)
Time and Space Between Us (Book 2)
Warrior of My Own (Book 3)
Begin Where We Are (Book 4)

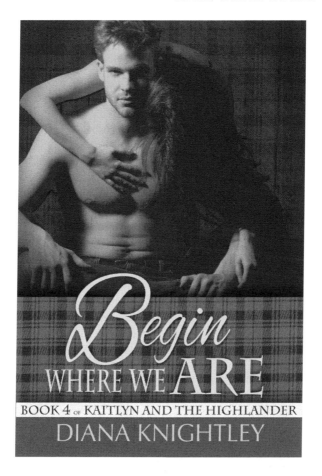

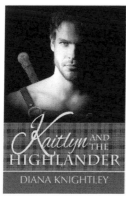

Can he see to the depths of her mystery before it's too late?

The oceans cover everything, the apocalypse is behind them. Before them is just water, leveling. And in the middle — they find each other.

On a desolate, military-run Outpost, Beckett is waiting.

Then Luna bumps her paddleboard up to the glass windows and disrupts his everything.

And soon Beckett has something and someone to live for. Finally. But their survival depends on discovering what she's hiding, what she won't tell him.

Because some things are too painful to speak out loud.

With the clock ticking, the water rising, and the storms growing, hang on while Beckett and Luna desperately try to rescue each other in Leveling, the epic, steamy, and suspenseful first book of the trilogy, Luna's Story:

SOME THOUGHTS AND RESEARCH...

Some **Scottish and Gaelic words** that appear within the books:

Turadh - a break in the clouds between showers

Solasta - luminous shining (possible nickname)

Splang - flash, spark, sparkle

Dreich - dull and miserable weather

Mo reul-iuil - my North Star (nickname)

Bidh thu a 'faileadh mar ghaisgeach - you have the scent of a breeze.

Osna - a sigh

Rionnag - star

Sollier - bright

Ghrian - the sun

Mo ghradh - my own love

Tha thu breagha - you are beautiful

Mo chroi - my heart

Corrachag-cagail - dancing and flickering ember flames

Mo reul-iuil, is ann leatsa abhios mo chridhe gubrath - My North Star, my heart belongs to you forever

Dinna ken - didn't know

A h-uile là sona dhuibh 's gun là idir dona dhuib - May all your days be happy ones

Characters:

 Kaitlyn Maude Sheffield - born 1994

 Magnus Archibald Caelhin Campbell - born 1681

 Lady Mairead (Campbell) Delapointe

 Hayley Sherman

 Quentin Peters

 Zach Greene

 Emma Garcia

 Baby Ben Greene

 The Earl of Breadalbane

 Uncle Archibald (Baldie) Campbell

 Tyler Garrison Wilson

 John Sheffield (Kaitlyn's father)

 Paige Sheffield (Kaitlyn's Mother)

 James Cook

 Michael Greene

Locations:

Fernandina Beach on Amelia Island, Florida, 2017

Magnus's castle - Balloch. Built in 1552. In early 1800s it was rebuilt as Taymouth Castle. (Maybe because of the breach in the walls caused by our siege from the future?) Situated on the south bank of the River Tay, in the heart of the Grampian Mountains

Talsworth castle - this is an imaginary castle, though I have placed it near Spittal of Glenshee in the highlands of eastern Perth and Kinross, Scotland

Kilchurn Castle - at the north-east end of Lock Awe (book 5)

The kingdom of King Donnan the Second. We don't know anything more... yet. But I suspect Magnus recognized one of the peaks.

ACKNOWLEDGMENTS

My Facebook page was kicking it for a while there. My friends and family weighed in on many questions I had about how Magnus would find the new New World. The conversation continued over in the FB group, Kaitlyn and the Highlander.

Thank you to David Sutton for reading and advising on story threads. From pointing out that Zach needed more depth to his character to noting that extra battery packs were necessary for the condenser, from how Kaitlyn might view the miscarriage to how the drones would be navigated, your insight was really, really helpful (and kept me adding things up to the last moment!)

Thank you to Heather Hawkes for beta reading, championing, being a long time friend and supporter, and for making the countdowns to Magnus's arena fights actually count down instead of up.

Thank you to Cynthia Tyler for excitedly reading, finding so many errors that I had to take deep breaths, (It's awesome how many you found, truly) and saying this, "Magnus's dad is an effin' psychopath!" Exactly. Also, when you said, "I only wanted to let you know that this whole passage, the message it imparts, is so freakin' wonderful," about the entanglements, you made me cry in the good way. Thank you so much.

Thank you to Jessica Fox for reading and advising. Your thoughts on Kaitlyn's character under duress were spot on. I fixed it, I hope.

Thank you to D. Thompson who has been reading ARCs for me, book after book after book, and is so helpful. And you're welcome for adding the reference to zombies.

Thank you to Carla Martin for helping me come to a decision about contracting those 'my's. I agree. They're outa here. I appreciate your notes so much.

Thank you to Kristen Schoenmann De Haan for reading and loving the progression of the story, but also my writing. You've been with me a long time, I'm glad you're still here.

Thank you to Liana McGuinness for helping me locate the small village near the imagined, Talsworth castle, in Scotland and being so active in the group. I appreciate it.

And thank you to Joshua Waier, for your advice on the big battle at the end, your choreography was right on and as I was writing it I just got so excited about it all. As Quentin put it, "... this is cool as fuck. A science fiction battle in a medieval castle."

Thank you to Kevin Dowdee for being my support, my guidance, and my inspiration for these stories. I appreciate you so much. And thank you for working with me on the battle scenes. That was awesome.

Thank you to my kids, Ean, Gwynnie, Fiona, and Isobel, for listening to me go on and on about these characters, advising me whenever you can, and accepting them as real parts of our lives. I love you.

ABOUT ME, DIANA KNIGHTLEY

I live in Los Angeles where we have a lot of apocalyptic tendencies that we overcome by wishful thinking. Also great beaches. I maintain a lot of people in a small house, too many pets, and a to-do list that is longer than it should be, because my main rule is: Art, play, fun, before housework. My kids say I am a cool mom because I try to be kind. I'm married to a guy who is like a water god, he surfs, he paddle boards, he built a boat. I'm a huge fan.

I write about heroes and tragedies and magical whisperings and always forever happily ever afters. I love that scene where the two are desperate to be together but can't because of war or apocalyptic-stuff or (scientifically sound!) time-jumping and he is begging the universe with a plead in his heart and she is distraught (yet still strong) and somehow, through kisses and steamy more and hope and heaps and piles of true love, they manage to come out on the other side.

I like a man in a kilt, especially if he looks like a Hemsworth, doesn't matter, Liam or Chris.

My couples so far include Beckett and Luna (from the trilogy, Luna's Story). Who battle their fear to find each other during an apocalypse of rising waters. And Magnus and Kaitlyn (from the series Kaitlyn and the Highlander). Who find themselves traveling through time and space to be together.

I write under two pen names, this one here, Diana Knightley, and another one, H. D. Knightley, where I write books for Young

Adults. (They are still romantic and fun and sometimes steamy though, because love is grand at any age.)

DianaKnightley.com
Diana@dianaknightley.com

ALSO BY H. D. KNIGHTLEY (MY YA PEN NAME)

  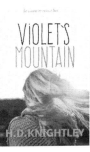 

Bright (Book One of The Estelle Series)

Beyond (Book Two of The Estelle Series)

Belief (Book Three of The Estelle Series)

Fly; The Light Princess Retold

Violet's Mountain

Sid and Teddy

Printed in Great Britain
by Amazon